Con Man

BASED ON A TRUE STORY

Con Man

The Story of Jack Stiles
and the Women Who Were His Victims

S. Hale Humphrey-Jones, Ph.D.

urlink
PRINT & MEDIA

Con Man

Copyright © 2024 by Hale Humphrey-Jones, Ph.D. All rights reserved.

No part of this publication may be reproduced, stored in a retrieval system or transmitted in any way by any means, electronic, mechanical, photocopy, recording or otherwise without the prior permission of the author except as provided by USA copyright law.

The opinions expressed by the author are not necessarily those of URLink Print and Media.

1603 Capitol Ave., Suite 310 Cheyenne, Wyoming USA 82001
1-888-980-6523 | admin@urlinkpublishing.com

URLink Print and Media is committed to excellence in the publishing industry.

Book design copyright © 2024 by URLink Print and Media. All rights reserved.

Published in the United States of America

Library of Congress Control Number: 2024924344
ISBN 978-1-68486-987-9 (Paperback)
ISBN 978-1-68486-989-3 (Digital)

14.10.24

INTRODUCTION

On May 8, 1996, my life fell apart. In one disastrous afternoon, I lost my career, my reputation, my soul mate, and my financial security. It was but a few days later that I began asking myself how could I possibly have been so stupid. Armed with a healthy education and a lifetime of information regarding the psyches of others, I had yet fallen victim to one of the oldest cons. Never had I imagined myself in the role of victim. It was unthinkable. It could never happen. It did. Then, I began to realize that, if it could happen to me, it could happen to anyone.

Writing my story began as a form of therapy, a way to cope with the pain and guilt over what my husband had done, and the role I had inadvertently played in his misdeeds. Once written, I began to hope that this book would serve to protect others from falling into a similar trap. Most of all, I sought a manner of restitution for the violation and betrayal my husband had inflicted upon his victims.

In addition to my personal experiences, many of the facts in this story were gathered through conversations with family members, friends, and other professionals as well as from letters, diaries, and documents. Some of the characters depicted here are composites. Names, places, dates and circumstances have been modified to protect the privacy of those involved. While this is a work of fiction, and many of the persons and places are products of my imagination, the basis for the story is real. I know. I was one of his victims.

He was led into the courtroom, his hands cuffed in front of him. Even in the rumpled orange jumpsuit provided by the Department of Corrections, Jack Stiles maintained his usual haughty composure. With an amused half-smile he scanned the room for the women. They were all there. He could feel them, all but Julie. Julie would always love him—never betray him like the others.

Deirdre, though, she was the most treacherous of them all. He spotted her immediately. Even with the dark glasses and gray scarf, there was no way she could hide that strawberry blond hair. She'd been his best. He'd really done a number on that one. After six years she still believed his story—until the last arrest.

With his back to the courtroom, Jack could still feel Deirdre behind him, remembering the first time he'd seen her. She was wearing a white cotton dress, somewhat casual for a professional, but crisp, almost pristine. When she looked up at him with those brown doggy eyes, he knew she was ripe for the picking. God, Deirdre was so easy.

Quickly, Jack's amusement turned to anger. She should still be with him, supporting him, getting him out of this hellhole. Instead, he heard she was filing for divorce. The bitch. He would fix her. She would be so sorry she had ever betrayed Jack Stiles.

DEIRDRE

Deirdre slid silently into the last remaining seat at the back of the courtroom. Peering through her dark glasses she could see the room was packed. Most of the other women were there. Julie, though, remained in California. As much as Julie hated Jack Stiles, she must love him more. Many of the women still loved him, in spite of everything he'd done to them. Deirdre wasn't one of those women, however. The only emotion she felt toward Jack Stiles was hatred. He'd nearly destroyed her.

She knew she'd taken a chance by coming here today. The prosecutor had warned her to stay away. They couldn't guarantee her safety. A lot of people wanted her in jail with him. They were convinced that she was his knowing accomplice. Her clients—their clients—wanted revenge on both of them. Most wanted her license, her money, and some even her life.

Not that there was any money, thanks to him. She was much worse than broke; she was indebted to nearly everyone. And now most of their clients were probably going to sue her.

She wished she could just run away and hide, but there was nowhere to go. Her friends had long since stopped talking to her. Even her best friend, Karol, had given up trying to talk sense into her. If only she had listened to Karol's warnings about Jack. Karol had gone so far as to threaten Jack, warning him to stay away from Deirdre. He just laughed in her face. After that, Karol gave up.

Her colleagues were embarrassed for her. She could tell by the way they looked at her that they couldn't believe she could be so taken in. Many believed she knew exactly what he was doing, maybe even helping him.

Then there were the reporters. They wouldn't leave her alone. The phone had rung constantly, until she'd finally yanked out the plug in frustration.

Nevertheless, she couldn't stay away. She had to see him sentenced. Like a burial, she needed the closure.

The soaring August temperature, combined with the emotional tension, created a stifling atmosphere in the crowded courtroom. Deirdre's scalp began to itch, but she didn't dare remove the scarf, or the tinted glasses covering her dark, but bloodshot eyes. Perspiration dripped onto her collar and waistband. The queasiness in her stomach, as it clenched into a familiar knot, threatened to lurch and empty that last swallow of coffee. Caffeine was probably the last thing she needed today.

She'd hoped the camouflage would hide her identity, but she knew Jack spotted her the moment he entered the courtroom. He looked terrible, but for once Deirdre felt no sympathy. He had lost at least ten pounds since his arrest and needed a shave. His dark hair, always impeccably cut, was scraggly and uncombed. The prison-issue, soiled orange jumpsuit was a far cry from the designer suits he usually wore. Nevertheless, he still carried that superior air, as though he knew something no one else could possibly understand.

In spite of the heat, Deirdre shivered in fear as she felt his rage reach out to her. Even handcuffed he had power over all of them. She forced herself to look away. She would not allow him to control her, not anymore.

Dr. Deirdre Warren was a professional counselor who had developed a con- sulting business after devoting over twenty years to a private marriage counseling practice, which she'd combined with a career in college administration. Jack Stiles had been her husband and partner in the counseling and consulting business for the past six years. Jack was supposedly the business manager. The truth was he never managed anything but the racing form.

Deirdre smiled as she thought of all the designer suits she'd given to *Goodwill*.

He'd begged her to come and get the cashmere sport coat he had on when they arrested him, but she couldn't bear to go back to that place again, not after that horrible night.

The call had come about 3:00 in the afternoon. She was in the middle of a meeting. As a mental health consultant, she reviewed policies, analyzed treatment practices, and assisted in program planning. She was reviewing a medication pol- icy with one of the psychiatrists who insisted on prescribing a controlled medication when Carlee, the receptionist, buzzed her.

"It's your husband, Dr. Warren. He says it can't wait."

"Jack, I'm in a meeting." Deirdre made no attempt to hide her annoyance. He probably wanted money to go to the track.

"You need to come home now," Jack demanded without preamble.

"What's wrong?" Deirdre was beginning to get alarmed.

"Just come home." The phone went dead.

Deirdre's mouth felt dry as she made a hasty retreat and headed home. Visions of catastrophes reeled through her mind on the drive that seemed eternal. She visualized her cat, Pax. having run out the front door into the path of a car, the house a burned-out rubble. None of her expectations prepared her for the reality she discovered when she walked in the front door.

Drawers were upturned on the floor, their contents scattered across the room. Files and papers were strewn everywhere. Her heart pounded in fear and confusion as men with guns on their hips tossed drawers and books onto the floor. Her husband, Jack, sat on the living room sofa. His hands were cuffed in front of him. He avoided her questioning eyes.

A man with thick dark hair and shaded glasses met her at the top of the stairs.

"Dr. Warren?" Deirdre nodded mutely. He stuck a card with his name and picture in front of her. "We're from the Justice Department.

We have a warrant to search the house." He slapped a paper into her hand.

Deirdre couldn't seem to take her eyes off the gun on the man's hip. The black, ominous object appeared to grow larger every minute. Her hands shook as she tried to read the paper in front of her. She couldn't get the alien words to focus. She kept seeing references to fraud and theft connected with the familiar names of clients. According to the warrant, their clients were charging Jack with embezzling their money. Deirdre kept looking at Jack. Why wasn't he talking to her?

"Is any of this true?" she finally asked him. Her lips felt glued together. Her eyes and voice begged for some indication that this was all a big mistake.

"Of course, not!" Jack seemed indignant. He rattled the handcuffs to convey his discomfort.

"Can't you loosen those?" She asked the dark haired man.

He shook his head. "They aren't tight."

"We need to check your car," the same man said.

She couldn't remember the name on his ID. Her head didn't seem connected with the rest of her. "What did you say your name was?"

"Murray," he answered grimly. "Bob Murray."

All the television shows flashed through Deirdre's mind. She should be out-raged, calling her lawyer, demanding an explanation, but she was too numb and frightened to do much more than nod. Bob Murray and Deirdre walked out to her car. She handed him the keys without comment. Bob opened the trunk. There was an empty cardboard box for carting books back and forth, and an old dog-eared paperback that Deirdre kept for reading when she was stuck waiting for appointments. The glove compartment contained an owner's manual, insurance card and registration. There was one box of pink tissues in the back seat.

"Do you have any other cars?" Bob asked. Deirdre shook her head.

Deirdre and Bob went back into the house. The other two men were still looking through files and papers. Deirdre now looked more closely at Jack, a look that demanded a response. He raised his eyes to hers, but they held no answers. Usually so expressive, his eyes were now clouded. He seemed almost bored.

Part of her was stunned and bewildered, but deep inside she had known for some time that there was something not quite right where Jack was concerned. She couldn't put her finger on why she had felt uneasy.

As a graduate student, Deirdre had studied handwriting analysis. She couldn't help becoming alarmed at Jack's constant doodles. They kept a note pad next to the phone to jot down recorded messages. The pad was covered with dark black arrows. Jack drew the arrows on the page corners of books, and other papers, as well. At times, the arrows seemed darker, deeper. Such doodles, she had learned were an indication of anger. Yet, Jack declared he felt no anger. He repeatedly declared himself a pacifist. Like many of Jack's declarations, pacifism seemed inconsistent with his actions.

Deirdre's internal alarm system was usually on target. In confusion and desperation, she had often tried to talk to Jack about her concerns.

Is there something you need to tell me, something I should know? She'd asked. Jack had taken her hands in his and looked into her eyes.

You need to trust, Darling. Not all men are like your ex-husband.

Jack was unlike most other people. He heard different music than the average person. Where he was concerned Deirdre usually found herself questioning her intuition. She stopped asking, and never mentioned the arrows.

Jack would never tell her the truth, anyway. He had a tendency to create his own reality. Over the years she'd learned he had the ability to lie with such ease and conviction, she was sure he believed it himself. She would hear him repeat stories to other people. He would elaborate, with intricate detail, seeming to ignore the fact that she had been present, and the events were nothing as he described.

When she confronted him, he would twist the events until she was unsure exactly what had occurred. In most cases, there was no need to lie, but Jack seemed more comfortable with deception than truth. In spite of his secrecy, how- ever, Deirdre never suspected he would do anything to harm their clients.

Over the years, Jack had developed an interest in couples communication counseling. While he was not a professional therapist, he had taken training with Deirdre in Couples Communication and was certified in this area. He seemed to be a natural, and it was obvious that the clients adored him. He had a manner of looking deep into their eyes and speaking with such a soft and gentle voice. A voice that inspired confidence. He had appeared to care sincerely about their problems.

Jack continued to sit calmly on the sofa. He looked bored, as though the entire experience was a mere inconvenience. He kept jiggling the handcuffs to remind Deirdre of his discomfort. Jack avoided looking directly at her, however, which was not in character for him. Deirdre began to realize instinctively that this was not just one big mistake. She felt a buzzing in her head. The floor seemed to tilt and she slumped into a chair.

During the search, the investigators pulled files and envelopes from under cushions and mattresses. There were IRS forms issued at the racetrack, forms indicating winnings of thousands of dollars. It was money Deirdre had never seen. This just didn't seem real. It couldn't be happening.

"Were you aware that your husband was winning this amount of money at the track?"

She shook her head. "I knew he won sometimes, but I've never seen these particular forms. I'm supposed to report all of his winning to IRS." She looked up at them, in confusion. "I guess he didn't give me all of them." She looked at Jack. He looked away. The buzzing in her head got louder.

"I think you're going to have to come downtown tomorrow," the one called Bob said. "We'll need an official statement." Deirdre nodded in agreement. She kept thinking things like this don't really happen. Do they?

The three men went into another room for a couple of minutes. She could hear them murmuring, but could not make out the words. When they came back into the room, two of them pulled Jack from the sofa.

"We're going to take him to Court #11 to be arraigned," Bob told Deirdre. "They'll set bail, then. You'd better follow us in your car."

For the first time in over an hour Jack spoke. "Can I kiss her goodbye?" he asked the men. They nodded.

Deirdre stood numbly while Jack brushed her lips. She felt herself recoil from the contact. She was grateful that the cuffs restrained his hands and he could not touch her. The action was like kissing a stranger. Or worse, a monster.

When they put him in the car, he looked back and said, "I'll see you in a few. minutes." He acted as though he was going to the store for bread and milk.

On autopilot, she followed the unmarked cars to Court #11. She was afraid to feel. The entire experience seemed surreal, like in a nightmare. When she arrived at Court #11, there was some confusion. Bob steered her back out of the building to the parking lot.

"They're backed up here," Bob told her. "We have to go to the prison detention center. They will arraign him there. You can follow us."

Again, she followed the car carrying the men and Jack. This time, they traveled into an area of town she had never seen before. The streets were all unfamiliar. Had this area always existed? The light was fading and she had to strain to see the car in front of her. She could no longer see the men inside or identify the color of the car.

Deirdre began mumbling the license number over and over. What if she lost them? She had to force herself to breathe, forcing each tiny bit of air through her dry, constricted throat. Seeking some remnant of saliva, she attempted to swallow, only to be met with the rising panic erupting like hot acid from her stomach. Her chest felt like huge rubber bands were being tied tighter and tighter around her lungs.

What if she lost them, she kept repeating? How would she ever get out of here?"

It seemed like hours before they finally arrived. In actuality, it had taken about forty minutes. They stopped the car in front of her and Bob got out.

"You have to park on the other side." He pointed to a nearly empty lot. "We'll take him in through the basement. You go in the main door." He pointed again. "They'll let you know when you can go into the court." He walked away before she could ask anything else.

Deirdre parked in the lot where Bob had directed her. There were no other cars or people in the lot. She locked her green Eldorado and walked as fast as her feet would carry her to the main door.

A big woman with greasy brown hair and a soiled dark uniform of an unidentifiable color stood behind a glass cage. She came out when Deirdre walked in the door. The name on the badge hanging around her neck read Martha something. Deirdre could only make out the Martha part. She didn't look like a Martha to Deirdre.

"You have to go through the metal detector," Martha barked.

Deirdre began to walk through the detector when Martha barked again. "You can't take that in." She gestured toward Deirdre's handbag. "You gotta leave it in your car. No money, no bag inside."

Deirdre walked back out to the car and stowed her bag in the trunk. When she returned Martha greeted her with a wand.

"Gotta check you out." She passed the wand down Deirdre's body. Deirdre caught a whiff of perspiration and stale tobacco. "Okay, go on through."

Deirdre walked through the detector, confused about why they needed both the wand and the detector, but sensed it wasn't wise to question Martha who had returned to her cage and was talking on the phone.

There was one other person sitting on the wooden bench, a small man in his twenties, who stared at his hands and mumbled quietly to himself. A metal table held a coffee pot, packets of sugar, and dried creamer. Deirdre looked at the two inches of mud-like coffee in the pot and decided to forgo the treat.

Her skin felt soiled and greasy. Spotting a ladies room she attempted to wash away some of the grime. Staring into the cold running water—there was no hot water—she washed her hands repeatedly. She would never feel clean again. Her stomach rumbled and she wondered how she could possibly feel hunger. She would not eat that night.

Leaving the bathroom, Deirdre sat numbly on a bench littered with papers and coffee rings. After what seemed like hours later, Martha came over and told her court was beginning.

Deirdre sat through two drug-related cases before Jack was brought in. He looked a little less composed, but still carried an air of confidence, as though this would all end soon. He looked at her with an expression of anticipation and something else. A warning? Deirdre knew Jack expected she would take care of all of this, something she did quite well and often. Jack had been in trouble when she met him; he was always in some kind of trouble. The problems were usually related to money, however. Jack never managed money well. But, this was different. Very different.

There'd been no time to hire an attorney. A young man, who looked to be in his twenties, sat beside Jack. Deirdre guessed he was with the Public Defender's Office.

"Your honor," the young man argued. "I recommend that Mr. Stiles be released on his own recognizance. He is a respected therapist and has responsibilities to execute." The words were spoken in a flat, unemotional tone. He was obviously tired. There was no fervor. This was not television.

The representative from the Attorney General's Office, another young man, was quite a bit more emphatic. "Your honor, Mr. Stiles is a career criminal. He has a history of jumping bail. He is a threat to the community. We ask that bail be set at $40,000, secured."

The things the prosecutor was saying about Jack seemed impossible. The nightmare was becoming more and more bizarre. She prayed she would wake up soon. She had lived with this man for six years. Those six years unwound themselves in her head. Red flags she had ignored waved menacingly in her mind. Why hadn't she seen them before? Who was this man she'd been living with all these years?

Jack was given permission to address the court.

"Your Honor," he cleared his throat several times, "I am a psychotherapist. My patients need me. It is essential that I be released so that I can attend to them.

This is a grievous error." He scowled at the prosecutor, cleared his throat again, and sat down.

Deirdre gasped. Somehow Jack's work in communication counseling had transformed itself into psychotherapy. Panic wound itself around her throat threatening to cut off her air supply. Would this never end?

The judge was an attractive and serious looking black woman in her forties. She looked at Jack for a moment and then down to the charges before her. "I am going to support the state's request for $40,000 secured bail." She stood and left the room.

The young man from the Public Defender's Office leaned toward Deirdre as Jack was being led out of the courtroom.

"What does that mean, secured?" Deirdre asked.

"It means that they don't want him to get out. You have to put up the entire amount, not just a portion. Do you want to post bail?

Deirdre shook her head, no. She felt cold. All of the doubts she had been suppressing about Jack Stiles were beginning to surface. Had she been wrong in supporting him all those years? She knew she couldn't raise such a sum of money, and at this point in time wasn't sure she wanted him out on bail. She needed to think.

As he left the courtroom, Jack turned to look at her. Get me out! The look said. This time the warning was undeniable.

Deirdre left the courtroom in a daze. She wanted air, but all she seemed to be able to do was gasp. The hour was very late. The three men she'd followed were nowhere to be seen. Dim yellow lights illuminated the parking lot. How would she find her way out of this grim, dark area? Looking around for someone to ask for directions, and seeing no one, she became frightened. Checking the back seat, Deirdre got in her car and quickly locked the doors.

Driving in circles through areas of the city she never knew existed, she finally located a sign directing her to the interstate. The interstate was familiar. The drive home was a blur. As she walked up her front steps, Deirdre wondered how she had managed to get home that night. It was well after midnight when she finally opened her front door, and she knew her life would never be the same again.

JACK

Jack Stiles always knew he was special. From the day he was born the nurses said he was perfect and beautiful. He had heard this story from his mother all of his life. He had to be special. It was his destiny.

As he grew, Jack proved them all right. He was special. When he entered school, he excelled. The fact that he attended a small, country school did not detract from Jack's pride in always getting the highest scores, especially in math.

Jack wasn't just smart. He was also well liked. Teachers beamed at him, and all of the students wanted to be in his presence.

And there was baseball. Jack played third base, his favorite position. He found the game exhilarating. Each hit, each catch, was like an injection of adrenaline. He loved everything about baseball. In fact, he was successful in all sports. No one told Jack that he was shorter than most athletes. After all, there was little competition in the small Western Pennsylvania town. Even the larger players lacked his coordination and agility.

Jack also had church, where he was the leader of his youth group. He would organize camping trips, work on fund raising, and initiate new projects. There was no activity in which Jack was not the central figure.

"My Jackie was born to be a minister," Jack's mother bragged to anyone who would listen. "He is a special boy, you know. Such a good boy."

After all, Jack reasoned, ministers are special people. He had to become some- one distinguished.

There were, however, two flaws in Jack's existence. When he was seven years old, his mother developed agoraphobia, and didn't leave the house for three years. Then, for no apparent reason, her illness just seemed to go away. She was able to leave the house with no visible anxiety. No one questioned why she had improved; they were all just relieved that the problem had abated.

During those years of his mother's illness, however, Jack had been called upon to be her contact with the world. While his father worked, Jack came home after school to be with his mother. She often told him how much she needed him to be with her.

If he went outside to play, he would hear her call, "Jack, stay where you can hear me. I need you to be close." Jack never resented staying nearby. It was important that his mother need him.

It was during the years of his mother's illness that Jack began to draw the arrows. He would trace the deep, dark arrows in all of his notebooks. Sometimes, when no one was looking, he would stare into space, his pupils narrowed to small dots, the color darkening like the arrows. Then he would flash his engaging smile, as if he had a secret, he would never share.

Jack's mother bragged about her wonderful son to everyone, but if he slighted her, she would withdraw her love from him, often for days. She refused to hug him or talk to him and to tell him he was her special boy. Jack dreaded these periods and would avoid doing anything to anger her. He would tell her only those things that he knew would make her proud.

While he was dusting for his mother, he inadvertently knocked over one of her favorite music boxes, breaking it beyond repair. She had collected music boxes since childhood. As he tearfully confessed, she stared at him with a look of disappointment, a tear sliding down her left eye, as if he had killed her beloved parakeet. Then she went into her room and closed the door. She didn't speak to him for days after his confession. There were no hugs or praise. Jack felt abandoned. After that, if he made a mistake, he would cover it up. She was never to know that he had erred in any way. His arrows became deeper and darker.

After his mother recovered from her agoraphobia, Jack began to play baseball. She went to all the games to cheer him on. He was happiest when he could hear her yell his name from the benches.

The second flaw in his life was when he discovered that his family was poor. Mr. Stiles worked hard as a carpenter, but he never made much money. Jack resented the idea that his mother wore clothes that were less stylish and cheaper than those worn by the mothers of his classmates. He avoided bringing friends home because his small house was shabby compared to theirs.

At night, Jack began to fantasize about a father who was educated and wealthy. When he met Dr. Vine his fantasy father image was realized. In addition to being a general practitioner, Dr. Vine was a Quaker who volunteered his time as a Scout leader. Through Dr. Vine's volunteer efforts, he and Jack formed their alliance. Dr. Vine's own son had been killed at an early age, so he emotionally adopted Jack. Jack appeared to be everything Dr. Vine would have wanted in a son, and Dr. Vine was certainly everything Jack wanted in a father.

In his ongoing daydreams, Jack imagined that Dr. Vine was, in fact, his father. He often referred to himself in private as Jack Vine. Dr. Vine taught Jack to play chess. Together they listened to classical music and discussed philosophy and religion. Jack felt that he deserved a father like Dr. Vine.

When Jack became ready for college, he demanded his father send him to an Ivy League school. Mr. Stiles had saved every cent he could in order to provide an education for his very special son. In addition, he took out a mortgage on the home that he had built with his own hands. When Mr. Stiles presented this money to Jack, he did so with great pride. But Jack was distraught. He could never attend a top school with this amount of money. Jack had excellent grades, but the top schools were extremely competitive, and their applicants were among the brightest in the country.

The smile Jack gave his father as he took the money was forced. He gritted his teeth so hard he cracked one of his molars. Still smiling, he retreated to his room where he had his first vision spell. Clutching the money, Jack felt his body become very hot. Anger toward his father surged through him in searing amber tongues. Why was he born to this useless family? As he gasped in impotent rage, the left side of his vision began to darken. In the next few moments it spread across his entire field of vision until there was nothing but darkness.

Fear now forced Jack to focus away from the anger. A voice inside kept telling him he could control these feelings. Counting to himself, he gradually slowed his breathing until the heat in his head and body began to dissipate. His field of vision began to widen until, after about an hour he could see clearly again. He was going to have to be careful. He couldn't lose control like that again. Suppose someone saw?

Jack swallowed his pride and anger and accepted the money from his father, but it wasn't nearly enough. Jack was forced to attend a good school in Philadelphia that offered a commerce and engineering program, which included co-op opportunities. Jack's parents were pleased, but Jack's true dream was to be a physician, like Dr. Vine, not an engineer. His disappointment grew exponentially as the months wore on.

In addition to his deep disappointment, college and Philadelphia were culture shocks to Jack. He was far from special there. The students came from all over the world and many were as smart or smarter than he. Most were from wealthy backgrounds and were comfortable with the luxuries that left Jack in awe. Jack's clothes were bought from discount stores and lacked the designer labels flaunted casually by his classmates. The world around him failed miserably to acknowledge Jack's uniqueness. In fact, in his new environment he was less than unique. He was mediocre.

Jack would watch those around him with seething envy. They didn't deserve their wealth and privilege. He was the special one. It would all be his, somehow. Jack's blackouts became more frequent.

In his second year, Jack joined a fraternity that reinforced his frustration and embarrassment over his background. Jack would hide the lunches his mother sent back with him following weekends at home. He was humiliated by his parents and made excuses when they wanted to visit him. He didn't want the brothers to know he came from a poor family. When he spoke of his father, he described Dr. Vine.

Spending money was limited. While the other fraternity brothers would buy expensive sport coats and take dates to fancy restaurants, Jack was limited to the one pair of chinos and one coat he saved up for a whole year to buy.

In his sophomore year, Jack met Helene. She was beautiful, Italian, with thick dark hair and a Sophia Loren figure. Just being with Helene made Jack feel important, and he liked the way the brothers looked at him with envy.

Helene soon tired of their long walks that served for dates, however. She told him that she wanted to go to the restaurants where the other frat boys took their dates, and she wanted presents. Jack didn't want to lose Helene. She was his big status symbol. He needed to find a way to get money.

The fraternity house had a pool table, and Jack quickly discovered he had an aptitude for the game. A good eye and a natural agility helped, but most of all he won, time and time again, because he didn't drink. The brothers were drunk every evening. Jack hated alcohol because it dulled his edge. He preferred coffee; avoiding anything that added to the depression he fought constantly. Pool was an instant high. He loved the game, and he loved the money he made playing it. It seemed to Jack that the brothers seldom noticed their losses, but to him the money made the difference between being nobody and being special. With his winnings he bought clothes to emulate the brothers, and began to take Helene to expensive restaurants. He even managed to obtain a credit card. Jack was a happy man.

No matter how well he did in school, though, Jack Stiles always felt shabby next to the brothers. Long walks, daydreaming about his future began to interfere with his classes. Indulging in fantasies about returning to Philadelphia as a famous physician was more important than calculus. A degree in engineering was not what he wanted. Dr. Vine was a doctor. Jack had to be a doctor. That was the only career that would truly make him special.

ROTC had a program on campus, which offered Jack extra money. He also found he liked the discipline. Once again, Jack excelled. The recruiters were always badgering the students about joining the military. They made promises to pay for his education and make him an officer. Officers were special. The military just might be his ticket out of this drudgery.

In January of his last year in college, Jack completely stopped going to classes. "I've joined the Marines," he announced to Helene. "They'll make me an officer, and men will salute me. We'll get married and live in exotic places."

Helene was disillusioned. She had wanted a college man, not a Marine. Mr. Stiles confronted Jack about his decision. "Boy, what can you be thinking?"

His mother shook her head and turned away from him.

On one of Dr. Vine's visits to Jack, he tried to talk to him about his decision. Dr. Vine frequently visited Jack in Philadelphia. He would take him out for lunch in places Jack could never afford. They would smoke their pipes and talk for hours. Jack began smoking a pipe when he left home because it made him feel more like his surrogate father. People would look at them in admiration as the aromatic smoke curled about them. The pipe itself seemed powerful, giving him purpose as he packed it lovingly. Special people smoked pipes.

Most of their conversations were amicable. The two men agreed on most issues. When Jack announced that he was joining the Marines, however, Dr. Vine strongly disagreed with Jack.

"You're too sensitive," Dr. Vine argued. "The military is wrong for you."

Dr. Vine knew that Jack could not stand up to the constant haranguing and criticism, which was the hallmark of Marine training.

"You know how depressed you got when your English teacher criticized your essay last year? It will be a thousand times worse in the Marines."

For the first time, Jack ignored Dr. Vine's advice, refusing to listen to any of them. He entered the Marines convinced that they would all realize he was right someday.

Jack had no idea how stressful the military could be. Oh, he loved the discipline. He loved the spit and polish and the exercise. He was good at all of that, and he was at the top of his class. However, part of basic training was designed to eliminate one's personal pride. Jack's pride was already fragile. He needed to be affirmed, not ridiculed. Jack hated being humiliated. The spells were so frequent that a couple of the men suggested that he go to the infirmary. Jack didn't want anyone to know about the spells. He pretended to have heat exhaustion.

The final straw was Vietnam. Jack was obsessed with death, often dreaming about dying. He would wake up in the middle of the night drenched in perspiration, feeling suffocated, his heart pounding in fear. What if there was nothing after death, nothing but blackness? He began to question his own religious training about heaven and the hereafter. What if there was no God?

The thought of nothingness was too horrible to imagine. He was convinced he would die young, but he didn't want to hurry the event along. He felt a driving need to fully experience each day, knowing there wouldn't be many more. Years in the jungle and probable death were not for him.

He'd overheard some of the men laughing at guys who had declared them- selves conscientious objectors. The idea began to take shape in Jack's mind. Claiming devout pacifism seemed to be the only way he could avoid Viet Nam. He had always hidden his rage so carefully, that those close to him believed him when he said he was a pacifist. He wrote letters to his minister back home and to his congressman. His mother sent letters to local politicians, as well. However, since Jack had volunteered for the Marines, his claims were not justified. Pacifists did not join the Marines. No matter how hard he tried, the idea wasn't working.

When it became inevitable that he was to board a plane for Southeast Asia within the next few days, Jack went AWOL. Pretending to go to the latrine late at night, he slipped quietly off base while the others slept. Dressed in dark clothes, he managed to avoid the guards at the gate.

Jack naturally assumed he would get sympathy and help from his family and his old fraternity brothers. The brothers wanted no part of him, however, and threatened to turn him in if he showed up again. There would be no sympathy there.

Next he visited Helene. She screamed at him hysterically, and swore he had ruined her life. Her shrill cries alarmed her parents, and Jack quickly left her house.

Jack was afraid to go home. His picture was on the evening news as a deserter. The FBI was looking for him. Mr. Stiles was humiliated and could not bear to speak to his son. He kept asking himself what he had done wrong in raising Jack.

After a frantic phone call from Jack begging for help, his mother and Dr. Vine met him in the parking lot of a diner in PA. They gave him some clothes and money, and promised to continue to seek help getting him conscientious objector status and amnesty, but his time was running out.

Dr. Vine and some of the Quaker community members finally helped Jack cross the border into Canada, where he was granted refugee status. At first, Jack was grateful to be safe, but working dreary jobs for meals soon wore thin.

Jack quickly learned to live on his charm and wits. People were more than willing to assist. He was perceived as a hero, standing up for his deep anti-war beliefs. Most helpful, however, were the pool halls.

Jack supported himself playing pool. Soon, he expanded his gambling efforts to playing cards. Once again, card players were often drinkers, giving him an edge. His mathematical acuity made poker his game of choice.

A new dimension began to creep into Jack's gambling, however. He began to lose. The irony was that he was defeating himself. The phenomenon was first apparent at the pool hall. He had been winning steadily for hours and was experiencing his usual adrenaline rush. Then he noticed his palms growing cold and clammy, and his hands starting to shake. Queasiness developed in the pit of his stomach.

Taking risks with his shots, he tried more difficult angles. He started losing and couldn't stop until he had lost all of the money he'd won.

At first he thought he was sick, but the phenomenon occurred more and more often, usually after he had won a great deal. He started to play games with himself to see just how much he could win before he would begin to lose. He never thought to stop playing when the spell hit him. He needed to find other resources for money. But most of all, he needed an identity, something that was special.

Jack's long conversations with Dr. Vine had included much discussion of poetry and poets. Jack had learned one thing about poets. They lived lives that were different from the overall population. Poets were special people, not bound by social constraints. Jack decided he was meant to be a poet. In fact, this was his true destiny. Everything that had occurred in his life had pushed him toward that destiny.

He began to call himself "Jack Vine," and he told people he was writing a book of poetry. This persona was particularly appealing to women, who gladly supported him in his endeavors, both emotionally and financially.

Bright, pretty women were his preference. They all shared one quality—they didn't know how pretty or how bright they were. Most gladly traded their money and support for Jack's charm and attention, and gave him their hearts. One such woman was Sheila.

SHEILA

In the summer of 1969, Sheila Davis was touring Canada with two fellow teachers from Virginia. Sheila had recently started teaching eighth grade English, and this trip was the first indulgence she'd allowed herself since college.

Her big doe eyes and soft, warm brown hair attracted many men, but Sheila saw herself as plain and usually discouraged any male advances. At just over five feet tall, she fought a constant battle with her weight. Even a five-pound gain could make her feel obese. Nevertheless, today Sheila was feeling happy and excited. She was convinced that this summer was to be a romantic adventure, just like in the movies.

The three women were pouring over a large map spread out over the table in a Toronto coffee shop. Each had a different opinion about which route they needed to take to their next destination. Their discussion was soon interrupted by a male voice, obviously also American.

"Unmistakably, the music of American voices." The man smiled down at the threesome, but Sheila realized he was looking mostly at her.

"How sweet I roamed from field to field," the man quoted as he slid into the chair beside Sheila.

Sheila continued the line, "And tasted all the summer's pride, till I the Prince of love beheld."

"Have I stumbled upon a fellow writer?"

"Are you a poet?" she breathed.

"Of course!" My name is Jack Vine. "And you?"

"Sheila Davis." She laughed, reddening. "Just a high school English teacher. Blake is my passion, one of my favorite poets. I never tried to write myself. That I leave to you geniuses."

Sheila looked at him with eyes that glowed. She flushed as Jack slipped his hand over hers as she held it under the table in her lap. He gently stroked her wrist with his thumb.

The sky was dark by the time the four of them left the coffee shop. Sheila felt hypnotized by Jack's eyes, his voice, and his touch. When he spoke to her, he lowered his voice to a near whisper, as though everything he said to her was for her ears only. He kept his gaze locked with hers. When they all walked outside, Sheila realized that Jack still held onto her hand.

"Sheila won't be joining you." Jack addressed her friends in a voice intended to brook no argument. He pulled her closer, putting his arm around her waist. "We are going to share an adventure together."

He turned toward her, quoting T.S. Eliot. "Let us go then, you and I, when the evening is spread out against the sky."

'Do not ask, "What is it?" "Let us go and make our visit,' Sheila responded. How could Jack possibly know how much she loved *The Love Song of J. Alfred Prufrock?* Sheila wondered as she turned toward her friends.

Her friends, Cheryl and Marlene, stared at her with open-mouthed astonishment. "Don't be crazy!" They cried in unison. "You've only just met."

"Take the van. Pick me up on your way back. I'll meet you right here on August tenth at 5:00 p.m." Her voice had suddenly become so decisive, so deter- mined, they looked at each other and shrugged in resignation.

"If you need us," they pleaded, "call the hotel in Quebec. We'll check in daily for messages." As though in shock, Sheila's friends walked off toward the van.

Jack turned to Sheila. "We are the last of the romantics, you and I. Let us taste of the joys of love and walk together through a timeless adventure." They walked through the quiet streets to his room, where they talked of the lives of Shelley, Byron and Keats.

For hours Sheila and Jack shared their literary passions. She would start a line, and he would finish it. His knowledge appeared to know no limits, as he impressed her with stories of the lives of her favorite poets. They shared so much in common.

Just before dawn they began talking about themselves. Sheila shared her lonely past with Jack. She'd had only one sexual experience. At age thirteen, an uncle had raped her. The experience had been her secret, and afterward she feared all sexual encounters.

Jack listened attentively, holding her close while she cried. He stroked her body gently, touching her ever so softly for what seemed like hours until he felt the change in her breathing as she was transformed from fear and shame to desire.

When he entered her, it was without pain. Sheila felt only a throbbing inside of her that grew toward great convulsions of release. She knew then, without question, she would love this man forever.

Sheila stayed with Jack all summer. She didn't meet her friends on August tenth, but sent a note informing them that she was fine and not to worry.

The summer Sheila spent with Jack was better than any romantic fantasy she had read or seen in the movies. They went everywhere together. Jack even let her watch him shoot pool. When he lost, she was happy to help him out financially. After all, it had been hard for him being forced to leave his country. He was so brave, though, to stand up to the warmongers the way he had. In September, however Sheila needed to make a decision.

"Jack, school starts next week. What should I do?"

Sheila's money was running out. She couldn't teach in Canada, and she was starting to fear that Jack was losing interest in her. In the beginning he loved that she followed him constantly with her eyes and wanted to be with him all the time. Lately, however, Jack seemed to get irritated by her growing attachment to him. He used all of the right words, like "I love you. I adore you." He said everything, but "marry me?"

"You know I can't go with you," Jack reasoned. "They'll put me in prison, military prison. They could even execute me. We are at war. The sentence for desertion during wartime is death. I would gladly give up my life for you, but then we wouldn't be together."

Sheila quickly rushed to assure Jack that she would never ask him to risk his life. She knew the danger he would be in if he returned to the States. It was for that reason that Sheila had avoided telling him about the baby. She couldn't wait any longer.

"We have more than just us to consider now, Jack. I'm going to have a baby."

Sheila began to feel panic as she watched Jack's face. She couldn't read his reaction. He seemed almost angry, but slowly his mouth moved and a huge grin emerged.

"My darling, this is wonderful news. The best gift you could give me. You know how much I worship you. What could be better than a child, a product of our love?"

All that night, they spoke of children's names and made plans for their child's future. At dawn they both agreed that Sheila would return home. She would tell her family she was married, but that the baby's father was in the military on a secret mission. She would have their child in the comfort and safety of her family's support.

"I would give my life to be with you," Jack began.

"Don't even think it," she hushed him. "You aren't safe in the States. Your child and I will come back. Then we'll be together as a family."

"Forever," he breathed into her hair.

Saving just enough money for her trip home, Sheila forced Jack to take the meager funds she had left after withdrawing most of her savings over the summer. Kissing Jack for the last time, Sheila boarded a train for Virginia. She had no way of knowing that she would never see Jack Stiles again. Her multitude of letters would remain unanswered. No communication would ever be forthcoming from him.

After several months, Sheila finally realized that Jack Stiles had used her. The love and passion she had felt for him soured and then turned to hatred. Their child would never meet her father.

JACK

Jack was relieved to be rid of Sheila. Once her money was used up, she was becoming tiring and restrictive. It was fun for a while, trying to see how far he could push her. She probably would have done anything for him. The baby, though, that was a scare. The last thing he needed was a child to support. His new freedom created a tingling of excitement in Jack. There were new conquests, new adventures. Life was good for Jack Stiles.

Since his arrival in Canada, Jack had connected with many of the expatriates who had found their way to the Canadian borders. Most of them were evading the draft. Many feared for their lives if sent to Viet Nam. A few, however, were idealists who strongly believed in the concept of pacifism. To them, this was an unjust war. Our political policies were evil and they shared a common enemy, the United States Government.

Jack was viewed by all of them as a hero. Not only had Jack protested the war, but had made the ultimate stand. He deserted the Marine Corps. Jack's status enabled him to move about in this group with a great deal of financial support. Many were more than willing to give this brave man some money to fund his ongoing battle against the warmongers.

Even the brightest glow, however, will begin to tarnish after a time. Jack discovered that he could stretch his hero status only so far. In the pool halls, was exchanged freely, but most expected it to be repaid. Once the money crossed Jack's palm, however, it was never returned. Staying in one place too long began to prove dangerous for Jack.

A group of expatriates had gone to Mexico. Word came back that they could easily disappear, particularly if they spoke Spanish. It was possible to get a flight directly to Mexico City without having to change in the States. The tourists, Jack was told, had money to spend on gambling, and one could live quite cheaply there. Jack had always excelled in languages. Once in Toronto, he alternated easily from English to French. Spanish would be no problem for Jack Stiles. Two months after sending Sheila home to have his child, he boarded a plane to Mexico.

While in Mexico, Jack Stiles met Julie.

JULIE

Julie Marshall stretched out on the chaise lounge and breathed in the warm rays of the Mexican sun. This was her first vacation as an adult without her parents. She was twenty-one years old and had recently graduated from the University of Toronto as a music major. Her plan was to teach music. Her secret ambition, however, was to sing. This was a dream she had shared with no one.

Performing in public seemed completely out of reach to Julie. The problem wasn't a lack of talent. Her voice was fine, and she knew that. The problem was her self-image. She saw herself as an ugly duckling, particularly next to her glamorous and beautiful older sister, Jaclyn.

Julie's sister was two years older and had always been the family star. She had been homecoming queen and married a successful attorney. Jaclyn had also majored in music, but her focus was on her marriage and social life.

While Julie had excelled in school, it was in a quiet way. She would bring home her grades without fanfare, while all of Jaclyn's accomplishments were broadcast throughout the family. Julie never attempted to compete with her sister. She did nothing to enhance her cute, freckled-face looks. She hid her green eyes behind a pair of thick glasses, and pulled her curly, auburn hair into a tight ponytail. Make-up was never considered. Why bother? She thought her petite frame was just too ordinary to bother to enhance with fashionable clothes.

Normally, she lived in jeans and sweatshirts. Today, however, she had borrowed a bikini from one of the women in her travel group, and pulled her hair loose from its rubber band. Julie was the kind of young woman who spent most of her weekends alone, but not due to a lack of interest on the part of potential suitors. Julie's shy manner was interpreted as snobbish, untouchable. She had the kind of intense sex appeal, though, that was enhanced by the fact that she was totally unaware of the impression she made. Today, however, that potential would be noticed.

A lot of men had paid attention to Julie during her vacation. Their clumsy attempts at charm did not impress her, however. Nor was she interested in those who would treat her, as she had always been treated, fragile and pure. Julie had a second secret desire. Just once in her life, she wanted to experience excitement. Only three days were left of her vacation. Just when it seemed as if it might not happen at all, she noticed Jack watching her from one of the second story terraces.

Julie had noticed Jack earlier. He walked around in a Marine fatigue jacket. She knew he was one of the expatriates who had found their way to the various Mexican cities and resorts, escaping the draft, or as in Jack's case, deserting.

She and her family had looked down on the draft dodgers and deserters that had begun trickling into Toronto. As a group they seemed arrogant and demanding. What right did they have to expect her country to support them?

Yet, there was something exciting about him, even dangerous. Maybe it was the way he carried himself, so sure, so different from the others and from her. He kept his brown hair short in spite of the style, which was for longer, unshorn locks. He was obviously not governed by convention. Julie wasn't surprised when he suddenly appeared in front of her.

"I'm going to owe a guy fifty bucks unless you walk away with me right this minute," he began.

Julie laughed and held out her hand. "And if I do walk away with you?" She countered.

He pulled her gently but firmly from the chaise until they were nearly touching. "Then I win much, much more than fifty bucks," he whispered into her ear.

Julie flushed and felt a thrill of excitement. It was really going to happen, she thought.

"Which way is your room?" he asked.

"Why not your room?"

"Oh, I don't have a room here. I've been visiting friends. A week long poker game, actually." He looked at her and grinned. "I won."

For a moment he looked like a small boy who had caught a high fly and was bragging to his mother. His gray-green eyes sparkled and seemed to reach inside her. Julie felt her stomach flip over.

When they entered her room, Jack picked up the phone and ordered a bottle of champagne and two glasses. "We'll do this every year," he told her as he nuzzled his face in her hair, "for the rest of our lives." Then he kissed her and didn't stop kissing her until the champagne arrived. He paid for the champagne with a wad of cash.

"When I saw you out there, I knew. My heart leapt." He held his hand over his heart with such a look of sincerity that Julie was forced to stifle the giggle in her throat. He wasn't kidding.

"No, Julie, this is not a joke," he whispered as though he had read her mind. "This was meant to be. We belong together. You feel it too, don't you, Baby?"

"Yes," she moaned softly. "Oh, yes!"

At the age of fourteen, in a clumsy, brief act of curiosity in her cousin's barn, Julie had lost her virginity. The experience had left her totally unfulfilled. She knew that someday it would be different. With Jack it was. He was very skilled in lovemaking. He seemed to know she craved passion, not tenderness. When he thrust into her, he wasn't gentle and she didn't care. Her body met his with each movement. When they finally fell apart in exhaustion, Julie knew she could never leave this man.

They talked all night, between bouts of lovemaking. Jack told her of his plan for their lives.

"Life is very short and I will die young. I know that for a fact. So I must wrench every ounce of pleasure from each day. We will live without the constraints of society. We have no need for the ritual of marriage. We are married now. I married you the moment you took my hand at the pool."

Jack told Julie he was a fugitive, wanted by the FBI for deserting the Marines. The danger made him all the more exciting. He was everything she had never known in her life and had always dreamed about. He was dangerous and thrilling. He spoke of his pacifism and philosophy about money.

"Most people live their lives working every day in dreary jobs so they can save their money," he said. "They die without ever experiencing pleasure. They don't know what to do with all their money. I do. People invest in me, in my talent."

Jack told her he was a poet. Julie knew little about poetry, but she was immediately certain that Jack was brilliant.

"In three days, I have to go home," Julie said. "I want to spend every moment with you."

Jack smiled. "Baby, we will make every moment a lifetime."

Julie spent those three days with Jack. They walked on the beach, talked, and made love. Julie told Jack of her ambition to sing and of her sister, Jaclyn.

"You are so beautiful, but you see yourself as plain. When you begin to believe in your beauty, others will notice, too. Look into my eyes. What do you see?"

When Jack looked at her that way, Julie knew she was, indeed, beautiful.

"Now, we need to do something with your clothes," Jack announced. "My beauty, you hide your looks behind those jeans and pony tail. Let your hair down. Come with me."

Jack took Julie to a beauty salon where he directed them in her make over. The transformation astonished Julie. She kept looking into the mirror to assure herself that it was really she.

"Now for the clothes," Jack insisted. "Let's get rid of those rags." He took her to a small, expensive boutique where again he sent sales clerks scurrying to meet his demands. Julie followed his directions with glee.

"Here," he said. "Forget the jacket. Wear the dress alone. You have beautiful breasts. Don't hide them."

He listened to Julie sing. His eyes glittered with appreciation. "You really are talented. We'll get you lessons, and you will sing."

Julie called her parents in Canada after that first night, and had a tearful pleading conversation with them. She would not be returning with the group. She told them all about Jack and how she planned to live with him forever.

"Please Mama, try to understand. I love him so. I have never been so happy before."

"Julie, sweet," her mother pleaded, "we have raised you to be responsible, not to live without marriage. And with such a man, a draft deserter."

"Mama, our love transcends rituals and rules. We are special. We belong together." Julie had already begun to parrot Jack's philosophical propaganda.

"Julie, you're our daughter. We will always love you, but this man is not welcome in our family or in our home. Do not bring him here, ever. When you come to your senses you can come home. Your father doesn't wish to speak to you right now."

"But, Mama." Julie dissolved in tears as the connection was broken.

There would be no acceptance of Jack from Mr. and Mrs. Marshall. They were a conservative couple. Mr. Marshall was a successful businessman and owned a large department store. Mrs. Marshall was active in charity work. She had been raised to believe that the role of women was to provide a proper home and to be socially accepted by all the *right* people. None of their friends would tolerate the deserters and draft dodgers who had immigrated to their country. The Marshalls had high expectations for both of their daughters. The likes of Jack Stiles was not part of those expectations. Most important, however, living together without the benefit of marriage was unheard of in the Marshall family.

Julie sobbed for hours as Jack held her and soothed her with his quiet voice, telling her of their life together and the joy they would experience. When her sobs abated, he made love to her until she forgot her parents protestations and thought only of him.

The wad of cash in Jack's pocket was quickly depleted, and they had to check out of the hotel. Julie and Jack traveled in Mexico, using Julie's savings until all the money was consumed.

"They sent me this credit card when I graduated," Julie offered. New college grads were always sent credit cards without question. Jack took the card from her greedily. They took it to a bank and made the maximum cash withdrawal. When they reached the limit on that card, they found that getting additional cards was easy. They ran up all the limits until that resource expired. Then things began to get tough for Jack and Julie.

JACK

Jack ripped a check from the checkbook with a flourish and smiled warmly at the impatient woman in front of him.

"You two month late," grumbled the small woman. Mrs. Hernandez, their landlady, was trying to learn English and insisted Jack and Julie communicate with her in their language. This was a relief to Julie, who spoke fluent French but could not seem to pick up the nuances of the Spanish language. Jack, however, loved to show off his multilingual talents whenever he could.

"Now, Elena," Jack teased, "You know I would never forget you. I was busy writing. Artists get lost in their work."

"Artists, hah," Mrs. Hernandez scoffed. "I see you next month—on time." She stomped out slamming the door in her wake.

"Jack, you know there's no money in that account," Julie whined.

Jack sighed. Here we go again. Naturally, the account was Julie's, the third checking account she had opened in Mexico. Each time the bank began to bounce their checks, the couple moved to another city and opened a different account. Jack couldn't risk opening his own account. The banks tended to ask too many questions. He was, after all, still a fugitive. Jack had grown to relish his identity as a renegade. He felt special.

Jack kissed Julie's forehead. "My love, I will cover that check after tonight's poker game."

Julie had seemed to find their attempts to avoid paying the rent amusing at first. She would laugh with Jack and share in the intrigue of their evasive tactics. After a time, though, she began to complain. Her parents had always paid their bills, she told Jack repeatedly, and this didn't seem right to her.

Jack recognized that look of disapproval on Julie's face. His face clouded over as he formulated his response.

"My father worked all his life to pay bills on time. What did it get him? Nothing." Seeing her look unchanged, he altered his approach. "Baby, baby, everybody lives on credit now. Do you think your sister and her new husband paid cash for that house they just moved into? Most people live way above their incomes. It's the American way."

Jack's tactic with Julie was to confuse her. He twisted logic until he knew she began to believe him. Then, he would whisper in her ear as he stroked her body, lulling her hypnotically. He knew she was so in love with him, she wanted to believe him.

Whenever Jack's juggling of funds began creating anxiety in Julie, Jack would talk to her about how special their lives were. They were above the mundane existence her parents and sister supported. Didn't she want excitement, he'd ask? Surely she never wanted to live like the establishment.

"Oh, I forgot to tell you," Julie blurted. "Enrique was looking for you. The check you gave him came back. He looked mad."

"Damn!" Jack was counting on getting some more money for tonight's game. He began to pace, which he often did when his plans for getting money to gamble fell through. He needed other resources. The time had come to meet some new *friends*.

Jack used Julie's beauty to attract people. While she was shy, Jack was confident and gregarious. People were lured by Julie's physical presence, but they were soon enchanted by Jack's charisma. Most people were more than willing to sponsor this lovely and charming couple who were living lives of true artists and nonviolent advocates.

They would sit in cafes and restaurants and strike up conversations with affluent people. The story was usually the same. Young lovers forced to flee from their country because of their political values. He was a poet striving to exist. She was his beautiful and talented lover.

Jack would entertain them and charm them. Often Jack and Julie found themselves as houseguests for weeks on end.

In between benefactors, Jack made money by gambling, mostly cards. Often he lost, and sometimes heavily. Covering the checks on time became harder and harder. When the check juggling system began to fail, and they couldn't cover the checks fast enough, they had to keep updating their supply of supporters, while beginning to avoid the old ones.

Jack was also finding it harder and harder to avoid the people to whom he owed money. Some of them shrugged the loss off as a bad investment or an entertainment expense, but others got angry—very angry. Things had begun to close in on Jack and Julie in Mexico. They couldn't go to the States. There was only one choice. They would return to Canada.

JULIE

In 1973, Julie returned with Jack to Toronto. Julie's parents refused to acknowledge them as a couple. They made it clear that Julie was free to return to the safety and security of her home whenever she abandoned Jack. Leaving Jack was out of the question for Julie. He was her soul mate. She could never leave him. At least in Canada she could work.

Getting a teaching job was difficult for Julie; they asked too many questions. In 1973, Toronto was still very conservative. They frowned on co-habitating couples. Teachers were expected to be role models for the children. So Julie went to work in a clothing store. Her looks drew customers. She didn't need a hard sell. She did quite well.

Since their return to Canada, Jack had started going to the racetrack. It seemed that the more money Julie made, the more Jack gambled. She was afraid that Jack was changing. The poetry that he'd loved so much was seldom ever dis- cussed. He almost never wrote anymore.

"What about your poetry, Jack. You haven't talked about it for a long time. I don't even see the typewriter. Where is it?"

"Oh, I pawned that. I'll get the typewriter back next week when I win."

Julie seldom questioned him, but poetry had seemed so important to his life. "Do you think you might be counting too much on the race track? Horseracing takes up so much of your time."

"Oh, my innocent love. Poetry has nothing to do with typewriters and paper. Poetry is written in the mind at all times and at all hours.

Shelley and Keats didn't write on schedule. They spent their hours filling their lives with pleasure. When the impulse hit them, they would write—often in the middle of the night. Poetry is not something you can order up like a rack of dresses. Some poets spend years not writing a word."

Julie was far from stupid, but she loved Jack totally, and anything he did was wonderful with her. She would listen in fascination to his tales of great poets and other famous people. There was no one as brilliant and exciting as her Jack. He was her love.

As time passed, however, Julie could not get past the anxiety of their ongoing financial insecurity. The dissonance between her personal value system and the one that Jack promoted caused great stress. True, she yearned for excitement, but she had not comprehended the amount of tension that excitement would bring. Julie had constant stomach pains, and began taking tranquilizers. Jack told her that she was just sensitive.

In 1973 Julie began her diary.

Days of turmoil and mental exhaustion. Jack took our last few dollars to the track and lost. We are down to one subway token. Hard to believe—not a cent, but money really doesn't matter. We are together and happy and that's all that's important. Made love twice last night. We're never too tired!

I was upset. Yesterday was my birthday. Jack had won $40 at the pool hall, but lost again at the track. Then Jack surprised me with a new pantsuit, scarf, and dress for my birthday. I cried. Suddenly he made me feel as if the most important thing in the world was for us to be together in spite of everything. Never said where he got the money. Made love on the sofa and then again in bed.

Delicious.

Had to take $10 from petty cash today, as we have no money again. Know this is wrong, but don't know what else to do. Don't have $ for rent, which is even worse. Returned the gifts for my birthday. I knew we couldn't pay for them. Very distraught. Jack wasn't there when I got home. He came in after I was in bed and slid in beside me. He said, "Daddy's here, Daddy will take care of you." Then he put "Sam" between my legs and everything was all right.

A very embarrassing incident. A man came to work today and delivered a writ. I started to cry; it was just too much. Earlier this week, Bell Canada had to garnishee my wages again. Jack had refused to call the landlady, so she told us we were going to have to leave at the end of next week. Two more checks came back. This puts us in an even worse position. My nerves are frayed and I think I may be pregnant. That will make Jack happy. He wants a child so. He will be 30 soon. I want to give him a child. Made love only twice this week. Jack says I'm not as responsive. Better watch it, Julie! What would you do if Jack left? Can't bear to think about being without him.

Often, when Jack and Julie were out together, they would see children with their mothers. Jack would strike up a conversation with the children, particularly little girls.

Do you know why you're so pretty? Jack would ask. They would shake their heads.

Can you do this? Jack said as he extended his index finger. The children nodded that they understood.

When someone asks you why you are so pretty, you do this. Jack would take the child's index finger and point it toward the mother.

The child would giggle, and the mother would blush. Julie watched in envy. If only she could give Jack a child. They could be so happy. Maybe Jack wouldn't spend so much time at the track.

Diary entry

Not pregnant, probably just as well. The demands of my job creep into my personal life and threaten my time to read and work and to sing. Work is postponing my lessons and eventually my ability to teach singing. I want children desperately, but feel afraid of our financial situation. Jack was not as happy as I thought he would be about the idea of a child. Seemed withdrawn the past two weeks. Relieved now. Starting to feel that I have no identity away from Jack. What am I without him? I'm only his reflection. Will I ever be able to do the work I want? How selfish of me. My life with Jack is the most important thing. Lovemaking better now than ever!

Jack began talking incessantly to Julie about his love of children, particularly during their lovemaking. He begged her to become pregnant.

"Make me a baby," he begged. "A beautiful little girl, the image of her mother."

When Julie finally became pregnant, however, Jack shocked her by insisting upon an abortion.

"Of course, I want a child," he insisted. "Haven't I demonstrated how much I love children? It's you I worry about. You're sensitive right now. It would be too hard on you to bear a child."

Julie insisted that she could handle motherhood, but much of what Jack said made sense. She was tired a lot, and emotionally overwrought.

"Later, my love. We will have our child later when you're stronger. Don't you see if anything happened to you I wouldn't want to live?

You're my life, Julie." A small tear rolled down Jack's cheek in confirmation.

Julie was touched and overjoyed that Jack loved her so much. She agreed to an abortion.

Diary entry

My arms, legs, hands, feet, head and mind remain the same, but something changed inside me today. I have come out less than I went in. I am no longer pregnant. I went to the hospital at seven in the morning. Jack drove me, and left me there. He said it was important that this be done on my own. I was given a wrist bracelet, and then was ushered to a room with two other women. I undressed and put on a backless hospital gown. It reminded me very much of the time I had my tonsils out. That same kind of gown and similar bed, only this time no Bozo lay beside me playing Rock-a-bye Baby. I wanted to cry and be that little girl again, but I know I cannot—not ever. An intravenous was started, with chemicals to reduce bleeding. We three lay waiting for the Doctor until 11:10. I was wheeled down the hall and into the O.R. There was a huge light above me and everything was very much as in Dr. Welby. White cotton leggings were put on me. My legs were put in stirrups, and I was given a shot of Valium, which made everything cloudy. A local anesthetic was injected into the womb and then I was seized with terrible cramps and pains. I could feel a sucking sensation and a rotating wiping feeling. More pains, and it was over. I didn't cry, but wanted to. The Valium made me nauseous. I returned to my room and Jack was there, smiling and trying to make me laugh. He had won at the track and brought me a present. We can't have intercourse for three weeks. Jack isn't going to like that. I don't think I will mind so much. There is a void, a feeling of indifference that I can't identify.

Julie was touched by Jack's tenderness with her following the abortion. He spent more time with her and went less often to the track. Julie knew Jack loved her and began to hope their lives would become more secure. Someday maybe she could get pregnant again.

JACK

In Canada Jack had discovered horseracing. The first day he walked into the track he knew this was his ticket. Money could be won faster and more efficiently at the track than with cards. All he needed was enough money to get to the track each day.

Jack's initiation to the track came completely by accident. Occasionally, he made money by tutoring math for students. There were always requests for tutors stuck on the bulletin board in the student union. For a brief time, he had even taught swimming, at a girls school. Once they discovered his credentials were phony, they asked him to leave. Lately, the tutoring jobs were dwindling, so he had, after hours of pleading from Julie, taken a part-time job driving a taxi. He fully intended to quit as soon as she calmed down.

One of his fares was an elderly woman who asked to be taken to the track. "I'll pay you fifty dollars to go with me," she said. Jack eagerly agreed.

The woman hated to go to the track alone. She struck a deal with Jack that he would go with her, sit with her, and then drive her home. Fifty dollars was a lot of money to Jack at the time.

She gave him his money in advance and showed him how to handicap. Jack won a hundred dollars that first day. He was certain his mathematical ability and keen memory could make him superior at handicapping horses. He easily remembered the horses past records at various distances and in different track conditions. This was his game!

A hundred dollars was a lot of money to Jack and Julie. That night they dined in style. He ordered in French and they ate escargot and drank white wine. Jack and Julie often ate in lavish restaurants, but as the guests of wealthy acquaintances. On those occasions they were expected to perform. This time they were alone. This was the life that Jack wanted. The racetrack could give them this life.

Strangely, the slightly seedy atmosphere of the racetrack, even in the clubhouse areas, never turned off Jack. There were numerous elderly people who appeared to spend all of their time in this venture. While many sported expensive watches and jewelry, he noticed most had shoddy footwear and worn cuffs. Many needed haircuts, but seemed oblivious to their appearance.

He could hear by the conversations and see by the number of torn tickets that, despite claims of winnings, most were losers. Somehow, in spite of the fact that losing was a common phenomenon, it wasn't a deterrent to Jack, but more of an inspiration. He was better and smarter than all of them. He could win.

All Jack needed was money to fund his daily ventures to the track. In Canada he had a whole new arena in which to begin his check cashing procedure. And in Canada Julie could work. Life was looking up again.

Julie's pregnancy was inconvenient. He liked talking about having children to Julie; it seemed to make her more responsive. He was convinced that all women wanted children. When she actually became pregnant, however, Jack nearly panicked.

He didn't want to leave Julie. She was beautiful and handy to have around. Most of all, she adored him, which made him feel special. A child would be a major roadblock in their lifestyle. It took a lot of convincing, but Julie agreed to an abortion. He needed to be more careful in the future.

For a few weeks after the abortion, Jack made a point of staying close to Julie. He wanted to be sure she wouldn't do something crazy, like go back to her par- ents. Soon, however, he returned to the track with a vengeance, spending more and more time at his new avocation.

When he wasn't at the racetrack, Jack loved to frequent hotel saunas. He could always befriend some clerk who would sneak him in. After all, Jack was special. He believed he deserved special treatment—and he usually got it.

Jack easily managed to get into the saunas at the smaller hotels, but he loved the big ones, although they were a bit trickier. He enjoyed pretending to be a guest of the hotel. Sometimes they even served him free drinks. Jack would wrap himself in their huge, soft robes and lounge by the pool after his sauna. Few thought to question this man who appeared so confident and comfortable. If they did ask for his room key, he would say his wife had it—she would be around shortly. He always used an annoyed tone that told them he was less than pleased. They quickly retreated.

The larger hotels were more of a challenge. He had his eye on one of the largest, most luxurious hotels in Toronto. The staff at this particular hotel was not easily intimidated, and guests were given a special key for entry into the spa area. Jack was going to need some assistance. When he spotted Doris in the coffee shop, he knew she would be his ticket.

DORIS

Doris worked at one of the largest, most lavish hotels in downtown Toronto. She had started as a desk clerk and worked her way up to management. Doris loved her work and couldn't wait to get to her beautiful, exciting job each day. The hotel had a luxurious spa with a sauna for its more than well-to-do guests.

Her daily routine was to come to work an hour early and sit in the atrium coffee shop. There, she could sip her coffee and breathe in the atmosphere of this special place that had become so valuable to her. It was on one of these occasions that she met Jack Stiles.

Short and slightly plump, Doris had mousy brown hair and watery gray eyes. She had a crisp, no nonsense, air about her, however, that belied her deep insecurity. Men seldom approached her, so she was surprised when this man with the soft voice sat down beside her.

"I hope I'm not intruding. You look so deep in thought."

"Well, no, I mean what can I do for you?"

"For me, oh not a thing. I just wanted to let you know what a magnificent job you are doing in this hotel."

"Why, thank you." Doris beamed with pleasure. "Are you a guest here?"

"A frequent guest, thanks to you. It is the little touches, don't you think, that make a hotel special?"

"I certainly do. I didn't realize, I mean, I didn't think anyone noticed."

"Well, I did, and I appreciate your commitment. Now, I've taken enough of your time. Good morning."

"Good morning." Doris watched Jack walk away. As she stared at the back of his dark head, though, all she could see were those eyes. This man—she never asked his name—had the most beautiful gray-green eyes she had ever seen. She wondered if she would ever see him again. But then, he did say he was a guest here.

The next morning, she recognized his voice immediately as he slid into the seat next to her.

"On duty already, I see."

"Not actually. I come here for my morning coffee. I just enjoy looking around when I'm not working."

"Good to see someone enjoy her work so much. Please forgive my rudeness. My name is Jack, Jack Vine. I'm a research physician. I travel back and forth from the States to review new medications."

Doris gazed into those eyes. They seemed different today. It must be the blue cashmere sweater. Today the eyes looked almost blue. She realized he was holding out his hand. She laughed, embarrassed, and took his hand to shake it. Instead, however, he held it between both of his for just a brief moment. Then, he smiled, those eyes sparkling.

"I didn't get your name."

"Oh, how silly of me. Doris, Doris Pickle."

"Did you say *Pickle?*"

"I'm afraid so. Most people just call me Doris P." Her face reddened even deeper.

"Must have been rough in school."

"Oh, yes!" She looked down at her short, well-bitten nails.

"I can see that's not your favorite subject. I shall just call you Doris P, for Perfect."

She shook her head. "I'm hardly perfect."

Jack took her chin and lifted it so that he was looking into her eyes. "That, my beautiful girl, depends on who is looking."

Doris smiled. She could still feel his hand on her chin. Such a soft hand, she thought.

"Now I have taken enough of your time for today. Perhaps tomorrow?" Doris nodded, still blushing.

Jack appeared every morning for two weeks. Then, one morning he wasn't there. Doris waited so long she was late starting her shift. Her disappointment was so intense that she kept disappearing into the ladies room to wipe away her tears. She chastised herself. How could she expect a man like that to really be interested in her? He was just being polite. She needed to get control of herself.

When he finally showed up, he seemed different, distracted. He took her hand in his, and she realized he was trembling.

"I must talk to you, Doris Perfect." His voice was gentle as always, but his face was somber. His eyes lacked their usual crinkle of a smile.

"Of course."

"No, not here. Will you meet me for dinner tonight? It must be somewhere private."

"We can go to my place. I'll make dinner."

Jack's face broke into a broad smile.

"I knew I could count on you, my perfect Doris. Thank you."

Doris wrote the address on a piece of paper and watched Jack walk away. Her excitement was nearly uncontainable throughout the day.

When Jack arrived at her apartment, he carried a small bouquet of flowers. They looked as though he'd picked them himself.

Doris thanked Jack for the flowers, putting them in a large green crockery mug. She sat down beside him on her large, stuffed sofa, handing him one of the two glasses of wine in her hand.

Jack smiled at her, took a sip of the wine, and then began to cry softly.

Doris was so alarmed she didn't know how to respond.

"Are you ill? Has someone died? What can I do?"

Jack wiped his eyes and looked at her with such tenderness she felt her heart would melt.

"My precious girl, I have lied to you."

She sat up straighter, suddenly alarmed.

"Please, no don't pull away from me. Listen to what I have to say. If you hate me afterward, I will understand."

"You know I could never hate you, Jack, but what is it?"

"Right after medical school, I joined the Marines. I wanted to save the lives of the poor souls who might risk their lives in the jungles of Viet Nam."

Seeing the confusion on Doris' face, Jack took her hand. "Please, just listen for a minute. It will all become clear soon."

Doris nodded.

Jack continued. "I was prepared to go into the jungles, but I was not prepared to fire a rifle, or to kill or injure another human being. You, see, Doris, I am a devout pacifist."

Her mouth formed a wide O as he continued his story.

"Shortly before we were to leave for overseas, I was told that I would be expected to carry and use a weapon. I refused. At first, they just intimidated and cajoled. Then, they threatened me. Finally, when I stood firm in my resolution three men took me into a room and beat me unconscious."

Doris gasped in alarm, but Jack held his hand up to let him finish.

"When I woke I was lying, face down in my own blood. My nose was broken and so were my ribs and my knee. I also had other injuries that are unspeakable. Doris, my dear, I'm sorry, but I can never complete the sex act."

He lowered his head and allowed a tear to fall onto her hand that was held tightly between his.

Doris leaned forward and kissed his forehead. "My poor darling."

"They assumed I was still unconscious because they left the door unlocked. I don't know how, but I managed to escape. The days afterward are a blur, but my father, Dr. Vine, and some other Quakers helped me across the border."

Jack stopped talking and took a sip of his wine. "The thing is, Doris, that I am not a guest in the hotel. I have little money because I continue to be a fugitive. They want me back so that they can execute me. I am considered a deserter."

By this time, Doris was sobbing.

"How can I help? What can I do?"

Jack smiled. "I knew I could count on you, my Doris perfect. I knew you had the character to understand."

Doris nodded.

"My injuries are very painful still, but I dare not take painkillers. My senses must remain sharp. I am on guard constantly. They search for me always. The only thing that seems to help my pain is the warmth of the sauna and steam. It provides some slight relief to the constant ache I have come to endure."

"You need a key to the sauna?" Doris brightened. "That is such a small thing. Of course, I can get one for you easily."

"Oh, my wonderful, kind girl. You are so special. If only I could love you the way I long to, but that is not for us I'm afraid."

Doris looked down. She had never had sex before. This affection was more than she had ever dreamt.

"I love you," she blurted. "I will do anything for you. Anything."

"Well, then," he smiled, "how about that dinner you promised.

The next morning, Doris gave Jack a key to the sauna.

Doris continued to see Jack in the morning. His visits were becoming briefer. He would sit with her, have a cup of coffee, chat briefly, and then slip off to the sauna. He was always friendly and warm toward her, but she sensed less affection. He was probably embarrassed about his revelation, she concluded.

A few weeks after Doris gave Jack the sauna key, Jon Michael, the head of security approached her. His expression was grave and cool, considering that they had known each other for over a year and had been quite friendly.

"Do you know that guy?" Jon pointed toward Jack as he exited the hotel, his hair damp from his last visit to the sauna.

"Well, I," Doris began to sputter, "I think he's a guest here."

"No, I checked. He's not registered here, but he comes in nearly every day. When I asked him, he showed me his sauna key and got quite indignant. Something about that guy makes me uncomfortable. I noticed him with you a couple of times in the morning, having coffee."

"Well, yes. I mean he does stop by and chat from time to time. I thought he was just being friendly. He complimented me on the job I was doing."

Um hm. Well, I don't know how he got the key, but the next time he comes in, he's leaving without it. We don't need to develop the wrong kind of reputation."

Jon started to walk away, but turned back to Doris.

"Doris, if you have anything to do with this guy, lose him. Fast." He walked away without waiting for a response.

Doris knew Jon took his work seriously. She might even lose her job. Her heart pounded at the thought. This job was her life.

Doris waited for Jack to come back to the hotel, but he didn't show up at his usual time. She realized that she had no way of contacting him. Jack had never given her a phone number or address. In fact, she realized, he'd never mentioned where he lived. A queasy feeling began to gnaw its way into her stomach, bringing a sour taste into her mouth.

Just as she was leaving her shift, she spotted Jack entering the sauna. Jon had just left. Could Jack have known Jon wouldn't be here now? She waited until Jack walked through the lobby and then followed him out the door.

She called to him twice. Jack seemed not to hear her. It wasn't until she grabbed his arm that he finally acknowledged her.

"Why Doris, I was so deep in thought. I didn't hear you."

"Jack, I have to talk to you. You're being watched by security. They've seen me talking to you. I could lose my job if they find out I gave you that key. I think you should stop using the sauna. In fact, I need to ask you for your key."

"Darling girl, don't worry about that rent-a-cop. I'll take care of him." Jack chucked her under the chin and walked off without giving Doris a chance to respond.

For a week, Jack didn't return to the hotel. Doris began to relax, thinking that he had understood what a problem he could be causing for her.

The next week, however, Jack returned. He smiled at her as though nothing happened. He didn't sit with her, but walked by and winked, as though they had some cute secret.

A few minutes later, she was paged by security. They were holding Jack in the manager's office. Jon Michael and the hotel's General Manager waited for her. They both looked angry.

"I tried to warn you, Doris. We gave you a chance to stop this."

Doris didn't know how to respond. Tears began to trickle down her face as she shook her head repeatedly.

"This man tells us that you offered him the key as a favor," Jon continued.

Doris looked at Jack, her eyes begging him to help her. Jack merely smiled.

Finally the manager spoke up. "I can't tolerate this, Doris. I'm afraid we're going to have to let you go. I'm sorry it had to come to this. If only you'd stopped when you were warned."

Doris stumbled out of the office, and into the lobby where she sank into one of the lobby chairs to catch her breath. Jack passed her, walking out the door without speaking. She followed, grabbing him by the arm.

"Couldn't you do something? I just lost my job. My job!"

"It's just a job, babe. Get another one."

Jack walked away without further comment.

Doris followed him with her eyes. He boarded a bus on the corner and disappeared. She never saw Jack Stiles again.

JACK

Jack was in a rage by the time he returned home to Julie. How could they evict him from their stupid hotel? Who did they think they were? They should be grateful that he cared enough to spend time there. That stupid girl, Doris, what a whimp she turned out to be. She should have taken a stand for him, told them he should be allowed to stay there. Who cared about her menial little job?

Jack continued to pace and rant until Julie, concerned that he was ill, tried to comfort him. He pushed her away, his face contorted. "Leave me alone, will you!" He staggered into the bedroom and slammed the door.

When he finally emerged, he acted as though nothing unusual had occurred.

While locked in the bedroom, Jack had another one of his spells. The spells scared him. He hated not being in control. Forcing himself to relax, he remembered how he had fooled that stupid girl, Doris. God, he was glad he didn't have to sleep with her. That injury idea was a stroke of genius, and he enjoyed pretending to be a physician.

Jack loved pretending to be someone else, especially a physician—that was his favorite. Often, when he wanted to cash a check, he allowed people to think he was a lawyer or a doctor. He would say that he was in a hurry and had run out of cash. His presence was so commanding that people were more than willing to cash checks for him.

Opening accounts with major department stores and buying expensive clothes for both of them was particularly enjoyable. He knew that Julie would probably end up returning hers, but he felt magnanimous when he brought home the huge packages. Naturally, he always kept his purchases, even if he couldn't pay for them. Jack loved the feel of expensive clothes, with designer labels and fabrics like cashmere and silk. He deserved these clothes. He knew Julie thought they should be paying the rent, instead of spending money on clothes, but that was for losers. They wouldn't stay in one place that long anyway. When the rent got too far behind, they moved on.

After a while, though, the complaints began to catch up to him. A subpoena to appear in court to answer a charge of fraud convinced Jack that Canada was getting a little uncomfortable. Jail had become only a few steps away.

Consequently, when the amnesty program in 1975 allowed Jack to return to the U.S, he did not hesitate. New territory was much needed.

The re-entry program required that Jack be trained to provide community service to compensate for the years he was to have spent in the military. After com-pleting his application for the amnesty program, he was informed that he would need to go to Indiana for training and debriefing.

While the government encouraged family participation, Julie was not his wife, and Jack wasn't ready for marriage, not even to her. She cried and begged, but he finally convinced her there was no alternative. He would need to go to Indiana without her.

At first, Jack was happy to be away from Julie. As beautiful and compliant as she was, Julie's clinging had been getting on his nerves. It was also cramping his style. Jack wanted some variety.

Jack hated the re-entry program, however. None of the women he met came close to Julie. He missed her devotion. He decided he wasn't ready to get rid of her—not yet.

During the months that he was away, he wrote Julie long, beautiful letters. He could not breathe, he wrote, until she was with him again. He knew that would keep her available until he was ready to send for her. It might be necessary for them to spend some time with his parents, and Julie could make that easier for him. Yes, he just might keep her—for now.

JULIE

Life for Julie was empty without Jack. She'd given up her life, her family for him. He was her reason for living. At night, she held his pillow and called his name through her tears.

Diary entry

I am nothing without Jack. He's my life. What will become of me if he doesn't come back for me?

After what seemed an eternity, however, Julie received the letter she was waiting for. Jack was sending for her at last. She was to buy a plane ticket to Philadelphia where Jack would meet her. For the days until her departure Julie was sick with excitement. What if he isn't there? What if he's changed his mind? What if his parents don't like me?

When the plane landed in Philadelphia, Julie had lost ten pounds. Her stomach convulsed in waves of nausea. Her throat was so constricted; the act of swallowing was nearly impossible.

As she stepped from the plane, Julie frantically scanned the area for Jack. When she didn't see him immediately, her heart nearly stopped in fear. Then, Jack stepped in front of her and she was in his arms. She clutched him tightly. She was whole again.

Jack kissed her, stroking her hair and hushing her cries, but he seemed to be holding back. After a few moments, she realized that Jack's parents were standing behind him.

Julie smiled at them through her tears and embarrassment. They put their hands out, but Julie rushed to hug them. They smiled at each other and at her. All her fears were immediately put to rest. Mr. and Mrs. Stiles accepted Julie with warmth and affection.

At first, Jack's parents just seemed happy to see him safe and happy. Julie felt, however, that there was something they were trying to say to her. When Jack and his father left the house to pick up some supplies from the store, Mrs. Stiles asked Julie to sit down and talk. Julie felt that the couple had planned this discussion.

"We love our son very much," the older woman told Julie. "We had hopes for Jack. We both told him not to join the Marines. We knew it was a mistake. Jack wouldn't listen. He never listens to us, especially not to his father. He's ashamed of us." When Julie started to speak, Mrs. Stiles held up her hand. "No, don't deny it. I know."

"Mrs. Stiles," Julie began, but the older woman stopped her.

"Please hear me out. This isn't easy. Don't let Jack talk you into anything. He's a good boy, he would never do anything really bad, but he does do things that get him into trouble. I don't know why. We tried to raise him the way God would have wanted us to. I don't know what we did wrong." Mrs. Stiles began to cry.

"You have a wonderful son. He's talented and brilliant." Julie tried to comfort the older woman. "I know he loves you very much. There's nothing to worry about."

Mrs. Stiles shook her head in frustration. "You can't see it yet, but you will. Just be careful." The woman stood, thereby ending the conversation.

When Julie tried to talk to Jack about the conversation, he announced that it was time to move on. That was fine with her. She liked the Stiles, but preferred to be alone with Jack, especially after their separation.

Julie was excited about their destination. Jack had been given several choices for his community service, but had chosen the one working with indigents in Southern California. She had always wanted to go to California.

They rented a car and drove to Los Angeles. Mr. and Mrs. Stiles gave them money for the trip, and Jack sold some of his books and a microscope to subsidize the journey.

The drive west was a fantasy for Julie. Jack was behind the wheel most of the time. She knew he preferred being in control, and felt uneasy when Julie drove. They began driving early in the morning, stopping at dusk. A camera in a pawn- shop captured their interest, and they took what seemed to be a million pictures.

At night they would find interesting places to have dinner, and then make love until they fell asleep, satisfied and exhausted. Julie had never known such happiness. She was certain that things would be better for them in California.

Along the way, Jack managed to locate a few racetracks. There was a big one in Illinois. They seemed to be zigzagging across the States. Jack was trying to visit the states that had racetracks, Julie realized. She didn't mind, though. Sometimes she went with him and he showed her how to handicap the races. On other occasions, when she was too tired, Julie would lounge at the motel pool until Jack returned. He was winning most of the time and both of them decided it was an omen. Things would definitely be good in California.

When they reached L.A., they found a resident hotel where they could pay by the week. Jack told Julie he had taken the car back to the rental agent. They didn't need a car. They walked everywhere or took buses.

The atmosphere was breathtaking. Julie had never been so happy. While Jack was at the track, Julie spent hours walking around Rodeo Drive, looking at movie stars, and window-shopping. She breathed in the excitement. L.A. was like no other world. Julie watched the beautiful, exotically dressed, people. There were no rules or limits here. She saw women in shorts with long coats, exposed navels and other body parts. Flesh was a form of dress in L.A. Oh, Mama, Julie thought, you would hate it here.

In the same breath, Julie realized that she never wanted to leave L.A. Someday she would be one of those beautiful, talented people. Julie hugged herself and smiled inwardly at the fantasy.

JACK

When Jack rented the car in Philadelphia, he'd used an assumed name, telling them he had lost his ID. He could always persuade people to do things that were outside the rules. When they got to L.A., he abandoned the car so they didn't need to pay. Why spend money unnecessarily?

Los Angeles was a playground for Jack and Julie. It was everything Jack had always wanted. He liked seeing movie stars and important people. They stood outside the academy award celebration and watched as the famous people stepped from their limousines. Being so close to stars made Jack feel valuable. California was where he belonged. He was important, too. L.A. would be a whole new vista for them, he told Julie, a new beginning.

Southern California, particularly Hollywood, was a new stage on which Jack could play out his role of young pacifist poet with his beautiful adoring love mate—wife was too *establishment*. He was already in violation of the amnesty rules under which he'd returned, since he wasn't completing his alternative service. Cleaning out homes in the San Joaquin Valley was not his idea of productive work. He lasted only two weeks, knowing all along that the track was much more to his liking. There were so many tracks to choose from in California.

Julie couldn't legally work in L.A. Jack had decided that it was time she pursued her singing talent. Having a talented and beautiful love mate was an even better draw for prospective *investors*. So he signed Julie up for singing and dancing lessons. He liked watching her practice. For the first time, he noticed, Julie seemed less inhibited, and able to let go and move her body. Julie was an extension of him, so he felt good about her accomplishments. He encouraged her to reach higher, to challenge herself with each exercise.

On the days Jack won at the track, their fantasy world came to life.

"You're home early," Julie squealed in delight. Jack stayed late when he was losing. An early arrival meant that he'd won and they were going to celebrate.

Jack spread the money over the bed in a green fan of twenties, fifties, and hundred dollar bills. "Get dressed, baby, we're going shopping, right after your surprise."

Julie gasped when they walked into *Sassoon*. She knew only the biggest stars went there.

"Make my baby even more beautiful than she already is," Jack said to the stylist as he kissed Julie's ear. "If that's possible."

Two hours later, Julie tossed her newly coifed hair and whirled in front of Jack, wearing tight new hip hugger, bell bottomed pants, circled with the silver belt they had purchased at the last store.

"We'll take it," Jack had declared with bravado. "Wear it, baby. I'm going to show you off."

Julie's eyes gleamed with happiness as Jack escorted her into the *Brown Derby*. He'd told her about the Derby—the natives just called it the Derby. He could tell by the way she gasped that she'd never imagined that she would actually be there. He noted the admiring looks people gave her as they were escorted to a table. She was his, so he was proud of her looks.

Jack flaunted Julie like a prized parrot, but she expressed no anger over such objectification, just the thrill of being a part of this sparkling life style, if only for a day.

The next day often found them eating tuna from a can, but on these fantasy days, they both refused to think about tomorrow. Today they were among the beautiful people. Today their dream was a reality.

That night Julie modeled the rest of her new clothes for Jack. She kept running her fingers though her hair, and he could tell she felt sexy. They pretended they were making an erotic movie as she slowly removed her clothes, piece by piece, and stroked her body. Jack was excited by her abandonment, knowing it was just for him alone. He was special to have her. Their lovemaking that night was better than ever.

Whenever they could, Jack and Julie went to expensive restaurants where Jack got to know the owners and managers.

"Hey, Vince," Jack would call to the owner. "What's good today?"

"Hi Ya, Shakespeare," they would answer since they knew he was a writer. "For you we make something special."

On days when they had no money, they were frequently allowed to eat free. Everyone believed that these two were special. They were proud to have this young poet and his lovely companion in their establishments. Someday, they all knew, he would be famous and they would add his picture to their gallery of celebrities.

Jack met people everywhere he went, and he usually borrowed money from them. Borrowing money was easier in L.A. because people were freer with their cash, and there was so much more of it. Jack's philosophy was that most people couldn't truly appreciate the money they had, and so it was better given to him. He knew how to live.

Often he met people at the track. Jack fancied himself an expert at handicap- ping horses. He convinced a number of people to pay him to place their bets for them. Many such people were wealthy, elderly women who spent their time at the track.

Jack was aware that Julie didn't really like the track. She had frequently pointed out to Jack the shabbiness that was always just underneath the superficial glitter.

There's always a smell, she had complained.

Jack thought that smell was excitement, but Julie said she thought it was fear. Jack didn't want to hear such logic. He took her with him less often.

The clubhouse was the only place to sit at the track. This is where the rich and famous went. Jack liked to hobnob with the famous and fleece the rich. Some- times he brought Julie with him to show her off. But mostly he preferred to work alone where he could enchant the elderly ladies.

MRS. HAVERLY

Mrs. Haverly went to the track on a daily basis. A woman in her early seventies, her husband had made a lot of money in movies many years earlier and conveniently died, leaving her everything. Mrs. Haverly was rich, bored, and lonely. She had been beautiful in her youth, and continued regular facials, never eating more than 800 calories a day, to keep her birdlike figure. Other than maintaining her appearance, however, she had never developed any interests, nor had she ever held a job. Charity work held no value for her. She liked the track.

At the clubhouse, Mrs. Haverly met Jack for the first time. Her limousine driver delivered her to the entrance each day, and she had her own table.

As she sat reviewing the racing form, she drew a circle around the name of a horse.

"I wouldn't bet on that horse," Jack leaned over her. "He has no breeding." "Which one would you pick?" She motioned him to sit down.

Mrs. Haverly won several hundred dollars thanks to Jack's pick. She didn't want or need the money, but she loved to win. She invited Jack to join her at her table for the rest of the day.

Jack soon became a regular guest at Mrs. Haverly's table. She was so pleased to have a companion that she began sending her driver for Jack.

When Mrs. Haverly finally met Julie, she was captivated with the beautiful young woman who reminded her much of herself at that age. The charming couple was a joy to have around. She began to look forward to seeing them, and felt sad when the day ended.

After only a few weeks, Mrs. Haverly asked Jack and Julie to move in with her. Jack had told her about their financial problems, and she had so much room. Why not? The couple would be entertaining for her during the long evenings.

Jack began to drive Mrs. Haverly to the track himself— why waste the limousine, he'd reasoned. She was touched by his offer. The driver, who was now free for the afternoon, had no complaints.

Together, Jack and Mrs. Haverly reviewed the racing form each evening. She was thrilled with the constant companionship. She felt protected by Jack, who kept the bloodhounds from taking advantage of her. Mrs. Haverly trusted Jack.

What would life be like for her when Jack and Julie left? She worried constantly about their inevitable departure, and began to create reasons for them to stay.

Jack could help her with her finances, she argued. Accountants couldn't be trusted. After all, look at all the stories in the papers about disreputable financial advisors. Money management was just too dreary for her. Would Jack please help her with this tiny matter? To her delight, Jack agreed.

JULIE

―⋈⋈―

For Julie, the arrangement with Mrs. Haverly was far from ideal.

"I want to go out alone tonight. We never have time together anymore," she complained, twining her arms around Jack's neck.

"Don't forget, baby," Jack cautioned, the old lady does pick up the tab."

"I know, but she's always around. We can't even make love until she goes to bed."

"She goes to bed early, my love. Don't worry, Daddy will make it up to you."

Julie suspected that their moving in with Mrs. Haverly was due to the fact that they were behind on the rent for their resident hotel. She didn't ask if the bill had been paid. Since she hadn't been working, she had less knowledge of their financial status. The ignorance helped her to feel less anxious. She'd hated worrying about money. Now that Jack was handling all of it, she could just close her mind and pretend everything was okay.

Sometimes, late at night, she would sense their lives weren't real. They lived in a pretty bubble that would burst one day. Then, to avoid feeling anxious, she would allow her mind to drift to her favorite fantasy. She was standing on a huge stage with pink lights, wearing a glittering long dress. Her hair was piled high on her head and she was singing, clear and mellow. The audience stood and applauded. The vision always relaxed her, and she would drift back to sleep.

Surprisingly, it seemed that Jack had money all the time now. Julie began to think that maybe he was right about the track. He must be doing well.

They opened a checking account and Jack cashed several checks. "The old lady paid me for driving her to the track," he told Julie.

Several weeks later Mrs. Haverly went to the track alone. Jack had told her that he was not feeling well. After the woman left, he went out and came back with a rented car.

"Pack everything as fast as you can," he told Julie.

Julie was afraid. She knew something was wrong. Jack had an intense, determined look on his face. He didn't seem to want to talk. Julie knew better than to question him now.

In silence, Jack put the luggage in the car. They drove south to San Diego and checked into a hotel. Jack left immediately. He didn't have to tell Julie he was going to the track; she already knew.

It was a long time before Jack returned, and he looked upset. Julie knew that look. Jack had lost. He had a knack for winning, but he equally had a penchant for losing, particularly when they needed a win the most.

Soon, Jack began to talk, slowly at first, and it all came out. "Okay, baby," he looked away from her. "We had no choice. We had to leave the old lady's house. She kept her checks in the desk drawer in the library. She asked me to get her checkbook and I saw the box of checks. She has so much money, she couldn't miss a little."

"Won't she notice when she gets the bank statement?" Julie began.

Jack shook his head. "I intercepted her bank statement so she wouldn't know."

"All those checks you cashed with her signature?"

"I signed her name."

Julie gasped and began shouting at him. He looked at her with such sadness that she forgot her anger and collapsed onto the bed. "What now?"

"We need to get the money back. My luck hasn't been too good."

So now Julie realized why Jack had been so tense. All the money was gone. Jack had not been doing well at the track. Mrs. Haverly had been getting impatient with him. Their time there had run out.

Julie was sick, and frightened. Very frightened. She cried and begged. "Please, Jack. Let's just get out of here."

"Baby, I know I can get the money back eventually at the track. I can't stop now. I've been on a losing streak. I'm due. Anytime now I'll hit big. You'll see. It'll be okay."

He also admitted that the rental car they had been using wasn't paid for. He had to get the money, or he would be arrested.

Jack kept writing checks and losing money. The hotel refused to accept a check for payment, so they had to leave in the middle of the night without most of their clothes. They checked into another hotel that agreed to take a check.

Diary Entry

Jack has to win at least $1000 at the track to get us out of this mess. Am feeling the strain. Jack is not conscious of the danger we are in. We are driving a car, which by now may be sought after by the police, we wear clothes we haven't paid for; we lost our apartment and possibly everything in it. When will it all end? Jack was late returning from the track. Please win. What will happen to me if he's arrested? What will happen to us?

Jack lost at the track. We have $5.00 left. Disaster. No alternatives at all. Who can we call? Where can we go? Jack called his Dad. Selective Service has been looking for him. His Dad refused to send money. Jack wrote a check for the room and checked out. Back to L.A. Maybe there someone will loan us some money.

It all ended today! Jack was arrested at 1 p.m. at a bank in Westwood. Mrs. Haverly had pressed charges of forgery.

Jack was handcuffed. The investigation began at the West L.A. police station. I was under suspicion. It was terrible, just like out of a movie. I was put into a detention room. My purse was searched, my picture taken. Jack was questioned. It was frightening. They had other charges to press, as well. Suddenly, it was time for Jack to be taken away. Jesus, I didn't want him to be left there alone. I called Mom and Dad Stiles, but there was no sympathy. Everywhere I went the advice was the same. Take care of yourself, Julie; don't be snowed by Jack anymore. I can't leave him. I won't leave him. He needs me. I can't stop crying. Called bail bondsmen, need $200—impossible. Found a room, only a few dollars left. Angel, from the Old World Restaurant, loaned me $50.00. What will I do? I can't sleep. I took a tranquilizer. I'm not sure how I can handle this. It all seems so unreal.

Jack went to jail for six months. Those six months were a blur for Julie. She got a job in a nearby clothing store. They didn't ask for work papers. If no one checked, she would be okay. She spent her days at work, and her nights visiting Jack, and waiting for him to come out. She was always tired and felt ill, like she had a chronic case of the flu. Julie soon learned that she was pregnant again. This time there was no question in her mind about an abortion.

Diary Entry

Sat in the OBGYN clinic at UCLA; I was alone. I was ushered into a small room. Abortion #2 began. They injected me with an IV of Valium and soon felt a bit high. The operation began almost immediately. Very much unlike my first experience in Toronto. It was extremely painful. I cried. A counselor was by my side trying to comfort and console. Two abortions was not the way things were supposed to go.

Jack wrote Julie long letters every day, proclaiming his undying love. The letters all read almost the same way:

> *My beautiful, precious darling. Each breath I take, each swallow of water is only bearable because you are there waiting for me. Nothing has any meaning without our love. It's everything. I can't believe that we're not together. I touch your hair in my sleep and hold your body, but when I wake there is only the lingering scent of your skin and I am, once again, in this living hell. My love, we will be together again and it will be different. I will make you happy, my darling, I swear on my life. I love you, forever!*

During their visits, Jack promised Julie he would change. "We'll get married. That will make your parents happy. I'll get a job. I can do it for you, my love, for us. It will be different. We'll be together always. I swear."

Julie believed Jack. She always believed him. She knew that he needed her.

They were married on April 17, 1978 in the Los Angeles courthouse. The wedding day was nothing like Julie had dreamed. There was no white dress. Instead, she wore a green pantsuit.

The beard Jack had grown made him appear grim. He seemed agitated and kept looking around as though expecting someone or something.

Julie asked a stranger to take their picture with a Polaroid. When the picture came into focus, Jack's eyes, the eyes that she had loved so much, looked like those of a trapped animal.

He still didn't have a job. But he was looking. Julie was certain he would find something soon. She hoped.

Diary Entry

Disappointed with Jack. He lied to me. He only paid $100 to the rent. Have lost much respect for him and he certainly must not respect me.

Julie continued to work, and applied for citizenship papers. "I need to take some time off," she told her music coach.

"My dear, you are progressing so well. You must not quit now."

She felt sad, but was too tired to care very much. Soon afterward she discovered the reason that she had felt ill for so long. Julie was diagnosed with lupus.

"You need to take care of yourself," the doctor told her. "Get plenty of rest and, most of all, avoid stress."

Julie laughed dryly. How did she avoid stress? She wondered. Julie began to crave stability.

They contacted Jack's parents in Pennsylvania and told them of Julie's illness. For her sake, they agreed that the couple could come to stay with them until Jack got a job. Jack and Julie left California in 1979 and returned to Pennsylvania.

In spite of all their troubles, Julie was sad to leave California. She felt she was abandoning her dream. She hated the road their lives had taken, but she loved L.A. She dreamed of living there under different circumstances. Maybe someday—Julie didn't completely realize that her fantasies had ceased to include Jack.

The trip back across country was much different than their last journey. There was little laughter, and they seldom made love anymore. Jack drove grimly for long hours. He and Julie didn't seem to have much to say to each other. This time there were no stops at racetracks. Jack swore to Julie that he had given up the track for good. He was going to take care of her. But she had to wonder.

The Stiles were welcoming to Julie. She was now their "daughter." And Jack, in spite of everything, was still their son. It was agreed that they would stay in their home, the house that Mr. Stiles had built himself, until Jack could get a job.

Jack left the Pennsylvania house each morning, ostensibly to search for work. Julie was feeling ill every morning.

"God please don't let me be pregnant again," she prayed. Would it be possible for her to have a child under the circumstances? She hoped Jack would be happy this time. Maybe a baby would make a difference.

"Out of the question," Jack ranted. You can't possibly carry a child to term now. You're sick. You know it isn't healthy for you to be pregnant now."

"I thought you wanted children," she answered. She had never told him about the second abortion. She felt it would be too painful for him.

"Of course, I do, darling. I'm thinking of your health. You know how much I love you."

"I guess you're right." She did feel weak. The thought of caring for a baby seemed overwhelming. At the same time, however, she didn't know if she could face another abortion. She had once longed to be able to have Jack's baby. It would be so beautiful, so perfect, she had once thought. Now, however, Julie was realizing that Jack's concern for her was less than sincere. Would the time ever be right for Jack?

This time Jack went with Julie to the clinic. He held her hand and whispered tender words. She looked at him with new eyes. She could see his mouth moving and heard the words of comfort, but the words sounded hollow. She noticed that his mouth seemed weak and pouty. Why hadn't she ever noticed that before? His words were warm, but his eyes were cold and hard, even cruel. She found it difficult to conjure up the deep and loving feeling she normally felt for Jack. Where was it?

When Jack brought Julie home from the clinic, he settled her in the bedroom and went out to get a prescription filled for her. He had told her he'd found a job in Philadelphia working as a manager in a Department store, *Wanamaker's*. He said that they gave him the day off to be with his wife because she was ill.

She realized that she had forgotten to ask him to pick up her other medication. The number for the pharmacy was in the address book that he kept inside the brief case he always carried around with him. When she opened the case, she saw a stack of tickets from the Philadelphia Park Racetrack. She felt dizzy. She had to sit down.

Jack called a few minutes later to say that he had to go into work, after all. There was no doubt in Julie's mind that Jack's work was the racetrack. He told her he would be back in time for dinner.

Julie went to the kitchen where Jack's mother was preparing a meat loaf. They spoke for about an hour and then Julie phoned her parents.

Using a loan from Mr. and Mrs. Stiles, Julie Marshall Stiles boarded a plane for Canada just minutes after Jack came home. She left a note, which read:

NO MORE

JACK

In April 1981, Jack Stiles received a petition of Divorce from Toronto, Canada. The following grounds were cited:

1. The Respondent was a compulsive gambler and never held down a job. The Respondent lived off the money that the Petitioner made, and spent all of the money at the racetrack as well as in other gambling vices. The Respondent would continually lie to the Petitioner about money, and stole from her purse. The Respondent would steal the Petitioner's paycheque, forge her name on the back, and cash it.

2. The Respondent encouraged the Petitioner to become pregnant, but after she became pregnant, his attitude changed completely. He pressured her into having an abortion.

3. Throughout the time that the Petitioner and the Respondent were living together and during the marriage, the Petitioner was forced to take tranquilizers, due to the conduct of the Respondent. Her health deteriorated over the past five years, due to a health condition, which has now been diagnosed as lupus.

4. The Petitioner states that because of this aforementioned conduct of the Respondent, continued co-habitation is intolerable and serves this divorce petition based on the grounds of mental cruelty.

Jack couldn't believe that Julie would actually divorce him. She was merely distraught over the abortion. The medication she'd been taking for her lupus had caused her to react irrationally. He kept expecting her to call to say that she was sorry and would be coming back to him.

Jack called her family's home repeatedly. Her father refused to allow him to talk to her. Julie refused to take his calls. He tried many ruses, including pretending to be Dr. Vine, one of her physicians. Nothing worked. The family changed the phone number. His letters were returned unopened.

In addition, Dr. Vine discovered Jack's ruse and was furious.

"My boy, I think I did you an injustice by inadvertently encouraging your independence from your father. You are trying to be someone you aren't, someone you can never become. Accept your family. They are good people. Never, ever use my name, and don't contact me again."

Jack wrote to an old friend that Julie liked and respected. He begged Chuck to intercede for him. Chuck wrote back:

> *It always seemed hard for me to believe that a reasonably intelligent person would put up with you for long. Whatever happened to the promise and potential that everyone bet on and lost, especially you, the biggest loser? I believe you are still searching for that person, too. I hope you find him.*
>
> *You speak of the essence of you, the pacifist. You who will not kill, but torture others by taking small cuts of the heart and flesh and step back with those blue/green eyes full of innocence. You tell us that if we really loved and cared about you, we would do this or that for you. How often did Julie do whatever for you? I am listening, appropriately, to Janis Joplin's song, "Take a little piece of my heart."*

The letter from Chuck formed a tight ball in Jack's fist. Cursing, he threw the wadded paper against the wall. There would be no help from Chuck.

The Canadian police had issued a warrant for Jack's arrest before he left. He'd just managed to escape incarceration when he returned to the States. He couldn't go back to Canada and convince Julie in person. Eventually, he was forced to admit that he had lost her.

As usual, the track served as an escape for Jack. He left in the morning and returned at night with the racing form. Without speaking to his parents, he went into his room where he remained all evening. His mother placed a tray of food outside the door each evening. In the morning it was usually gone. She could hear him pacing late at night.

Mr. and Mrs. Stiles allowed their son to remain in their home for several months because they could see how upset he was over losing Julie. When they discovered Jack had stolen their Visa card, things changed. Jack had taken their new card with the temporary pin number from the mail, and obtained cash advances on it in order to continue his gambling activities.

Jack didn't wait to be confronted by his father about the Visa card. He was certain the bank had contacted them by now. He left town that day, moving into a luxurious hotel in Philadelphia. He told the front desk his wallet had been stolen, and he didn't have identification. Jack used the name Jack Maine. After ten days the hotel began to ask for some form of payment. He stalled a few more days until they locked him out of his room.

By that time, however, Jack had other options. He'd met a woman in the coffee shop. She came in each morning, ate breakfast, and read the paper before work. She worked for a bank nearby. Her name was Christie. While she wasn't Julie, she was appealing, with dark Italian features, slender and attractive. She lived alone, which made her ripe to be Jack's next victim.

CHRISTIE

Christie had never been married. She'd been engaged to a man who had jilted her at the last moment. Consequently, she was somewhat insecure where men were concerned. When she met Jack, she was on guard at first, but his sincere and gentle manner quickly put her at ease.

Jack told her that he had run into some bad luck while waiting for his book of poetry to be published. The publication date had been delayed, and he had used all of his available cash trying to finish the book and now he was being thrown out of the hotel.

When he said he needed some time to transfer funds from his bank in L.A., Christie was more than happy to allow Jack to stay with her—temporarily. He stayed six months.

Christie's parents had died, and she'd been left a small inheritance. Living in a comfortable townhouse in the Society Hill section of Philadelphia, she worked as a bank account executive.

Cash was kept in a safe in Christie's bedroom. The money was for emergency purposes, but she seldom went into the safe. She told Jack he could help himself if he needed a little ready money. Jack graciously accepted her offer, but he kept a ledger with all he owed her, writing in each dollar, so that he could pay her back. She was touched by his conscientiousness.

Jack's story seemed genuine to Christie. She had also been an antiwar activist and had worked for civil rights. She believed in helping others. But more than anything she fell instantly in love with Jack Maine—or rather Jack Stiles. Each night he whispered wonderful, exciting things in her ear, and caressed her in a way she had never been touched before. She wanted nothing more than for Jack to stay with her forever.

Jack had an old checking account from Los Angeles. He wrote checks and asked Christie to cash them at her bank. She complied, but then he told her that she needed to hold the checks because there was some problem getting the funds transferred. She trusted that he would make the checks good. However, what she was doing was illegal. Christie decided that she would need to cover the checks herself.

That night when she arrived home, Jack was out. Christie went to the safe to take out the cash necessary to cover his checks. The safe was empty. She went to her bankbook and discovered that he had withdrawn several thousand dollars from her savings account as well.

As painful as it was for Christie to accept, she realized she'd been taken. That night, when Jack returned, she told him to leave the house.

"You don't really mean that," he argued. "I'll pay back the money eventually." Jack refused to leave; repeatedly telling her he would make it up to her.

When he left the house the next morning, Christie had the locks changed. Jack still refused to accept her decision to end their relationship. For two hours, he banged on the door, pleading with her to reconsider.

Christie watched Jack through a slit in the drapes. As she watched, she could see his face change and harden. She began to feel fear. It seemed like hours before he finally stomped away from the door. Slumping gratefully onto the sofa, she realized how close she had come to danger. She would be much more careful about talking to strangers in the future.

JACK

Life with Christie had been comfortable. Jack liked her and enjoyed her company. He particularly enjoyed her home with its expensive furnishings. Jack had quickly thought of the house as his home.

He knew she would be upset when she discovered the money missing, but he thought he could calm her down. Changing the locks was something he hadn't bargained for.

Certain he could convince her to let him in, he pleaded with her for a long time. After awhile, however, his pleading turned to rage as his vision blurred and darkened. How could she do this to him? She was nothing, just a bank clerk. She should be grateful to be near him.

Finally, Jack realized Christie wasn't responding. As angry as he was, he considered kicking in the door. If she could change the locks, though, she might be capable of contacting the police. He didn't relish another stint in jail.

Jack's control of Christie was obviously over. Time to move on.

Fleeing Philadelphia, Jack went to Delaware, a neighboring state where they had several racetracks. There, he met another woman.

Joan worked as a teller. She was a tall, large-boned redhead. Jack felt her instant attraction to him. He massaged her carefully, speaking to her seductively each time he visited her window to place a bet or to cash tickets.

As he expected, Joan was waiting for him when he left the track. He invited her for dinner, for which she paid, and then she asked him to her house.

Jack wasn't attracted to Joan, but he needed a place to stay, at least until he had a big win at the track. When it came time to charm her with his lovemaking, however, he found he couldn't perform. He told her he was still in love with his dead wife and needed time to get over the grief.

Joan seemed disappointed, but agreed to give him time. After several weeks, though, she began to complain. Flinging back the covers, she stood over him.

"If you don't make love to me tonight, I'm going to find someone who will."

Her demands were becoming tiring, and Jack was not overly impressed with the living conditions. He'd been thinking of moving on. "Do what you need to do," he responded.

Having second thoughts-he still hadn't had that big win—he turned back, softening his voice.

"Look, I'll be back here later. We'll have dinner and talk about it."

Convinced that Joan was mollified, Jack left the house and headed to the track. He had no idea his life was about to change.

JOAN

Joan fell hard for Jack. When he smiled at her she felt an urge that had been stifled for over a year. Her husband had dumped her for a younger woman exactly twelve months earlier. Her ego was fragile, but she yearned for another chance at romance.

He seemed to be making a point of going to her window to place his bets throughout the day. After the fifth or sixth bet, he introduced himself as Jack Vine. She thought he liked her.

After her shift, she quickly changed into an outfit she'd kept in the back just in case. This was definitely the time to wear such a garment. She pulled down the top of her peasant dress, revealing as much of her shoulders and cleavage as was decently possible. Dabbing lipstick on her mouth, and brushing out her long red hair, she rushed to catch him in the throng of people leaving the track.

Jack was standing at the exit smiling at her as though he'd expected her to come after him.

"I thought you might be hungry."

Trying to catch her breath, she nodded. Taking his arm, she realized she was an inch taller than Jack, and hoped it wouldn't bother him.

They went to a small diner and had burgers and beers. Joan drove and didn't comment on the fact that Jack didn't have a car. She didn't care. When the check came, Jack asked the waitress if they could break a hundred dollar bill. She shook her head.

Joan immediately offered to pay, and Jack agreed, promising to pay her back. He didn't tell her much about himself, but she could sense that he had problems.

When they got back in her car, she asked, "Where to?"

"How about your place?"

Joan couldn't believe her good fortune. This man was actually going home with her.

When they got in bed, though, Jack kissed her gently and said good night.

"I know you aren't the kind of girl who would go for a one night stand. I respect you. When you're ready, we can make love."

Joan felt like screaming that she was ready NOW, but felt silly. This man was treating her like a lady. How could she complain about such gentlemanly behavior?

Joan waited for a week before suggesting that she might be ready to have sex. Jack seemed pleased, but after a feeble attempt, was unable to get an erection.

At first, she was crushed, but then he told her about his dead wife and she understood.

"It's okay. It takes time to get over someone you loved so deeply. I can wait."

After a few weeks, though, the waiting became frustration. She wanted this man, but he seemed completely uninterested. Nevertheless, he stayed in her house and slept in her bed. What was going on?

Joan had an uncle who stopped by every week or so to see how she was. He had a cup of coffee or a beer, and then left, always stuffing some money in her purse. Joan saved the money, keeping it in a shoebox in her closet.

She told Jack about the shoebox, asking him if she should put the money in the bank. He laughed and said that no one would expect her to have such a sum in a shoebox. After that, however, Joan began to notice the pile of bills getting smaller. She asked Jack about it.

"Oh, sure, I borrowed a few bucks. I'll put it back, don't worry."

Working as a teller for several years, had given Joan a sixth sense. As crazy as she was about Jack, she began recognizing the signs of a con artist. She probably wouldn't have minded the money, but the sexual rejection was getting to be too much. After she confronted Jack about her sexual frustration, his reaction convinced her that she was being used.

Jerry, a friend of Joan, was a county cop. When she told him about Jack, he agreed to run a background check on him. Several warrants turned up in various names, including Jack Maine and Jack Vine. His real name, she learned, was Jack Stiles. Jerry asked her if she wanted to file charges and she agreed. Jerry called the police.

That night when Jack walked in the door, the police were waiting for him. "Are you Jack Maine?"

Jack tried to bluff. "No, you have the wrong man." He had reverted to Jack Vine when he left Pennsylvania.

They picked up his brief case and began looking for papers. They found several documents with the name Jack Maine printed on them. They were putting on the handcuffs when Joan walked in the door.

"Tell them this is a mistake," he pleaded.

"No, Jack Vine, or Jack Maine, or whatever your name is," Joan retorted. "You made the mistake. Get him out of my sight."

JACK

Jack Stiles was sentenced to seventeen years in prison, with the chance of parole in three. The Public Defender had advised him to plead guilty.

"They will go easier on you this way," he told Jack. You have no chance with a jury. All those women will bury you."

Jack was not aware that most cases sent to the Public Defender's Office were pleaded out. They simply did not have the time and staff to take even a small percentage of cases to trial. Usually the Attorney General's Office negotiated with them, compromising on an agreed upon sentence.

The public defender hadn't counted on Patricia O'Reilly. She was a tough and determined Deputy Attorney General who had no intention of letting Jack Stiles off easy. She gathered all of his victims together and built a strong case against him. When he pled guilty, she asked for the maximum sentence, combining each act to run consecutively.

When Jack heard the sentence, he shot out of his chair. "This is a mistake," he shouted.

The judge stood and walked from the room without another word. The Public Defender gently pushed him back in his chair.

"Don't," he cautioned. "You'll just make it harder for yourself."

"But, you have to do something. You told me they would go easy on me. What happened?"

The attorney was looking at his watch, and putting papers in his briefcase. He was finished with Jack. He nodded his head to the guards who began pulling Jack from the room.

"You have to do something," Jack shouted at the man's departing back.

Jack found prison much harder this time than it had been in California. For one thing, there was no Julie. In California Julie had visited him daily and put money in his commissary account.

The basics are provided for inmates: three meals, prison clothing, a bar of soap and one roll of toilet paper. In order to get toothpaste, shampoo, candy or extra underwear, it had to be purchased in the commissary. Friends and relatives put money on an inmate's account. If there was no money, there were no extras.

Jack had no friends, and his relatives didn't know where he was. Even if they had, Jack was certain there would be little help forthcoming. There was nothing in his account. They had let him keep his pipe, but he had no tobacco for it. He traded his desserts for tobacco whenever he could, but it wasn't enough.

The food was an unrecognizable glob. Most of the time he didn't bother trying to eat it. Coffee was watery and usually lukewarm.

Even if the food had been edible, the pushing and shouting made eating impossible. Sometimes, though, there were oranges or apples. Jack would sneak a piece of fruit into his underwear to eat in the relative quiet of his cell.

It was never really quiet, however, even in his cell. The noise was deafening twenty-four hours a day. No one slept. Radios blared during all hours, and the lights were never turned off. Inmates yelled at each other, and fights broke out frequently.

Jack would fashion a facemask out of a sock so that he could sleep a few hours a night. Even with the mask, sleep was difficult. The other inmates were a constant threat. They resented his pretentious manner and affected speech. He was threatened with hand crafted knives and other weapons, and beaten on two occasions. His biggest fear was rape. Many of the inmates were HIV positive.

Each time he got a new cellmate, Jack tried to make himself useful immediately to avoid potential danger, offering to help them rewrite petitions and fill out forms and complaints. He would even help them write letters to their lawyers or girl friends.

Jack got lucky. He was put in the same cell with Frank Lorenzo. Frank was a burly, red-faced man who had been convicted of murder. He was in for life. Frank was connected to the mob and had a lot of power. People put large amounts of money in Frank's commissary account. He lacked for little, even in prison.

Frank had a girlfriend, a flashy blonde who visited him regularly. But the visits weren't conjugal, and he was horny. He needed an outlet. Jack figured he was better off being Frank's *girl* than being gang raped in the shower. So Jack let Frank use him during those three years and Jack used Frank, too. Frank got money put in Jack's account weekly. Jack soon learned that prison could be tolerable if you had protection.

It was in prison that Jack met *Hawk* for the first time. Andrew Wentworth Houser was never called anything but Hawk. The name was given to him as a child because of his hawkish resemblance. Hawk's jet-black hair protruded up from his head in wing-like fashion, refusing to be tamed down. Tiny onyx eyes and a curved beak-like nose punctuated his lean, unsmiling face.

Hawk never smiled, and seldom spoke. It was rumored that he could kill a man or woman in seconds by pressing his thick thumbs against the victim's throat. Even the most powerful and unpredictable inmates left Hawk alone.

The first time Jack looked into Hawk's eyes, he felt a connection. Hawk was as cold and unaffected as Jack was full of rage. Jack bubbled with an inner fury and resentment, while Hawk was as inwardly cool and dispassionate as he appeared. Hawk's actions were motivated by pure instinct and necessity, without guilt, and completely unrelated to emotion.

According to prison legend, Hawk had killed his first victim at the age of ten. A class bully, whom they called Junior, made fun of him in the lunchroom. He called him a bird, told him to fly away, and took his dessert.

Hawk had made no effort to defend himself in the lunchroom. He waited for Junior after school, following him and his friends at a distance. When Junior's buddies veered off, leaving Junior alone, Hawk slipped up behind him and shoved a large kitchen knife between his ribs. He quickly removed the knife, stuck it in his backpack, and went home.

Hawk had made no effort to conceal his actions. When confronted, he coldly admitted the killing without explanation. He was sent to a detention school, where he learned the value of secrecy. Hawk felt no guilt about the killing. The boy deserved it. Bullies never bothered Hawk again.

Jack knew that Hawk didn't particularly like him. Actually, he didn't like anyone. But he was cunning. There was a technicality in his trial that could eventually get him released from his life sentence for murder, and Jack could help him. His lawyers were not cooperating, and Hawk found it hard to communicate with them. It was apparent that Hawk needed Jack to help get the papers filed.

Jack and Hawk bonded in a way Jack had never bonded with another human. It was not affection, but mutual respect. Jack knew that, someday, he would call on Hawk for help. Hawk was ready to repay the debt. Someday....

Shortly before Jack was given parole, Frank got religion. A lot of inmates became devout Christians or Moslems, particularly those who had committed violent crimes. Jack found that amusing, but he listened to Frank read the bible for hours at a time. There were no more late night visits to Jack's bunk.

During his imprisonment Jack read, listened, and learned. He learned how to deal, to trade, and to survive in prison. He learned, for one, that he needed to marry his next victim.

After three years, Jack was paroled into a work release program. The work release coordinator assigned Jack to work behind the counter at a local diner. The owner of the diner had a relative who was in prison and was sympathetic to the concept of rehabilitation. It wasn't hard work, and the customers were easily impressed by Jack's wit and humor. He enjoyed flirting with the female patrons.

Jack had to work during the day and report back to a halfway house at night. This program would continue for the next six months. He could go out for weekends, but only if he had a sponsor who would sign for him. The sponsor would keep Jack in his/her home, and the parole officer would call periodically to check on his whereabouts. If Jack wanted to go out during the weekend, he had to call and inform them where he was going and for how long. Not a pleasant situation, but better than the halfway house. There was no Frank at the halfway house. Jack had no protection there. He needed a sponsor.

When he met Deirdre, he knew she would be the perfect victim. He might even marry this one.

DEIRDRE

"You're getting grouchy," Karol warned Deirdre. "You'd better eat lunch."

"I don't have the time to eat," Deirdre snapped. "I have a management meeting in forty-five minutes." It was one of those muggy August days, and the heat did little to lighten Deirdre's mood.

"Yes, and if you go in this condition," Karol responded, "You'll be unemployed in an hour."

Deirdre's hypoglycemic moods were common knowledge. As her friend and co-worker, Karol reminded Deirdre to eat periodically. With her blood sugar in check, Deirdre was one of the most rational people Karol knew. But as a typical workaholic, Deirdre frequently worked through meals. The big red flag was when she snapped at Karol. The two had met just two years ago when Karol was assigned as Deirdre's office manager. Deirdre was Dean of a small community college, having taught psychology for several years prior to making the move into administration.

Karol's talent and skill were apparent to Deirdre from the beginning. Deirdre learned quickly to value Karol's creativity. In only a few short months Karol was promoted to Media Coordinator. The two became inseparable friends. Both dedicated to their work, they were often seen working late at night in the office or in a restaurant designing an ad campaign or discussing a new marketing strategy for the college. They worked in spurts of energy and ideas, often unaware of time.

Deirdre was extremely private about her personal life. The day her divorce was final, she took a few hours personal time for the court hearing, returned before lunch and removed her ring in the bathroom. Then, she put out a memo stating that she had legally changed her name back to Warren. There were no public tears and no further discussion in the office.

Karol was the only one to know when Deirdre's marriage finally fell apart. Together, they went apartment hunting during lunch and quietly moved Deirdre out of the house that had served as her home for the past twenty years.

Deirdre took little with her to this new life. Karol tried to stifle a laugh when she saw Deirdre's bed. "What is that?" She pointed to an armless, blue fabric chair.

Laughing, Deirdre flipped the chair open. "It makes into a bed, a small bed, but a bed. See?" The pitiful blue mat sat alone in the middle of the bedroom floor. Deirdre had learned over the years with Hank, to cover her pain with humor.

"Well, it's the only thing he didn't want. It was in my office," Deirdre said with a giggle.

Hank had frequently reminded Deirdre that he paid the bills and, therefore, owned the house and everything in it. Her money was such a *pittance* it hardly mattered.

You can't afford to have rights, he had told her when she wanted to move a sofa. *You're just a guest here. Don't ever forget that.* How could she?

Hank was a self-made businessman, a financial success, who had both coveted and resented Deirdre's education. During their first year together, Deirdre and Hank would sit for hours and discuss the movies they had seen. Hank loved to listen to Deirdre talk about the motivation of the characters. His opinions were often rough, but insightful. Deirdre appreciated the balance of their perspectives.

Most of Hank's friends came from working class backgrounds; few were college educated. Hank loved to show Deirdre off. He was proud of her intelligence, and encouraged her to continue her education.

After the first few years, however, he began to worry about the disparity in their interests and associates. Deirdre spent her time with academics. He would listen to her on the phone with them, laughing over things he didn't understand. He hated feeling stupid.

Hank complained about the time she spent studying. Desperately trying to make him realize how much she respected his business acumen, she told him that she couldn't create businesses as he did, academics was what she did best. He only seemed to feel good about himself, however, when he could belittle her for her Ivory Tower pursuits. *What do you know about the real world?* He would sneer.

While Deirdre tried hard to please Hank, she refused to compromise her values. A presidential election accentuated the conflict between them. As she stood alone in the voting booth she knew that her choice would anger Hank. She hated the hostility and coldness when he was upset with her. For a brief moment she considered pulling that lever that would make Hank happy. She could see his smile. Perhaps he would be nice to her for a few days. What was she becoming? Had she no scruples at all? In the end, though, she had voted her conscience and took the consequences. They were considerable. Hank was furious for weeks.

Several months later, Deirdre successfully completed the comprehensive exams for her doctorate. Her committee members were happy for her.

"Congratulations! So, who is the first person you're going to tell?"

"Oh, I was planning on putting an ad in the paper," Deirdre joked.

Making a quick exit, she ran to her car, fumbling with the car keys. Safely and privately inside, she began sobbing. This should be one of the happiest experiences of her life. Why wasn't she thrilled? Deirdre couldn't ignore the realization that the one person who should be sharing her joy and pride would, on the contrary, become increasingly bitter as the result of her accomplishment. Deirdre was not a quitter and she believed that marriage was forever. This, though, was not a marriage, she finally reasoned. There was no point in continuing.

Hank accused her of wanting to leave for another man. He had always been certain that she was cheating on him.

"Probably some bozo with a library card," he'd laughed derisively.

Deirdre ignored his insults and refused to take anything with her. He insisted she move within the week. She complied.

The year following Deirdre's divorce, Karol was the only one who knew how lonely and unhappy she was. Karol repeatedly tried to get Deirdre to go out and meet people, particularly men.

Deirdre felt safe only when she was working. In her work, she felt capable and secure with her abilities. As a woman, however, Deirdre felt undesirable and unattractive. Men her age, she argued, wanted teenage cheerleaders. She was over forty and had never been a cheerleader.

Deirdre was the kind of woman that men loved to conquer, but seldom wanted to keep. She did little to bolster their egos. The men surrounding her eventually felt impotent in her presence. Even if they succeeded in dominating her on the surface, there was always the sense that she was truly the one in control. They never stuck around for long. Deirdre's interpretation of this fact was that she was simply undesirable.

At forty-six years old, with strawberry blond hair and dark eyes that were just slightly more brown than black, Deirdre would have been curvaceous if she had been a few inches taller. As it was, the busty figure on her five feet two-inch frame gave her a slightly plump look. While she could appear totally in control, both in her role as Dean, and in her private counseling practice, her failure with men left her feeling personally undesirable and inadequate.

At Karol's insistence, Deirdre went once to a singles bar alone. She walked into the bar, ordered a drink, walked around the room, put down the glass and left. The entire time she felt sick to her stomach. Who needed such stress? Deirdre knew she would live her life alone.

On August 2, 1989, Deirdre and Karol entered a diner for a quick lunch and met Jack Stiles.

Normally impatient to begin with, Deirdre had no time for the long line in front of her. When Karol recommended they sit at the counter she agreed. Looking around in annoyance for a menu, she loudly requested one from the counter man.

"We don't give menus to customers," he retorted.

Deirdre began to sputter in frustration when she looked up into a pair of intense gray-green eyes with crinkling laugh lines at the corners. She had to laugh in spite of the situation. Karol stared in astonishment. People usually left Deirdre alone when she was in these moods.

She quickly learned the man's name was Jack Stiles. He wasn't really handsome. He was actually rather plain looking, short at five feet eight-inches tall, with straight, unremarkable brown hair. Still, he had a habit of looking into your eyes as though he could read your soul.

Friends of Deirdre's would later comment on Jack's eyes, saying that they were cold, but she didn't see it. Not then. Deirdre and Jack joked about the food and the service. His smile seemed genuine and friendly. He was obviously bright and witty. She ate only part of her sandwich, and then she and Karol left for their meeting.

"He was flirting with you," Karol joked. It had been a long time since anyone had flirted with Deirdre.

"He's probably married with five kids, teaches math in the winter, and is working to pay off a mortgage," Deirdre replied.

"Actually, he reminds me of you—a male version of you," Karol quipped. "But you're right about one thing, he sure isn't the run of the mill soda jerk. Maybe he owns the place."

"No, he told me the diner was owned by two young guys. I think he may just need the money. But, we'll never know."

That night Deirdre went out to the movies with friends. After the movie they wanted to get something to eat. Deirdre suggested the diner.

He was standing at the counter when they walked in. He smiled a quick greeting. Deirdre felt herself flush. She introduced him to her friends and asked him to join them if he could get a break. He did. When Jack sat down, he pulled out a pipe and asked if he could smoke. They all gasped. Deirdre, who normally abhorred smoke of any kind, couldn't respond. She merely nodded with a dopey smile on her face.

Several weeks earlier they had all three gone to a psychic for fun. The psychic had told Deirdre that she would meet her soul mate and that he would have one bad habit, he would smoke a pipe. Deirdre had a healthy skepticism about psychics, but this had to be more than coincidence. It seemed almost fated.

Deirdre went back to the diner often that week until, on Friday, Jack called her at work. He invited her to come to the diner at closing time so that they could talk.

She waited for over an hour until he finally came to her table at the back of the diner. "I'm sorry you had to wait so long," he grinned sheepishly. "We're not usually busy this late at night."

Deirdre watched while he packed his pipe. She waited for him to speak. He seemed nervous, almost boyish and shy.

"When you walked in the other night, my heart leapt."

A laugh formed in Deirdre's throat at the corny statement, but Jack looked so earnest and sweet, she merely smiled.

"I never thought it would happen again. The first time was with my wife, almost twenty years ago."

"Your wife?"

"She's dead," he whispered. His face took on a look of sadness. "Julie died of lupus. We searched for years for a doctor. We didn't know what was wrong. She was tired so much. It was terrible." Jack's voice broke and he didn't speak for a moment.

"Then, when I saw you, it happened again. I never thought I could love another woman after Julie. Oh, I know we've just met, but love works that way. That's why I have to be totally honest with you. I have to tell you everything. There can be no secrets between us, ever."

Deirdre was stunned. She knew she should protest. How could this man love her? He barely knew her. Yet, it felt so good to hear the words. It had been such a long time.

"I believe that we must do what's right," he began in explanation. "I have devoted my life to peace. It hasn't always been easy. People hate you when you threaten their values. It is easier to hate and to believe in violence than to turn the other cheek."

Deirdre started to speak, but Jack stopped her. "Please, darling. Let me tell you everything. If you hate me afterward, I'll understand. I'm a convict, on work release at this moment. In fact, I must return to the Krammer House in an hour. Three years ago I was arrested for protesting the nuclear power plant in Salem."

"It isn't against the law to protest," Deirdre responded, finally finding her voice.

"No, but when they want to get you, they can. I was accused of inciting a riot and refusing to pay my fine. I should have been released in hours. Instead I spent nine hundred and sixty-two days behind bars. It was unspeakable." He shivered and took a deep breath.

"How horrible. You don't have to talk about it."

"No," Jack took Deirdre's hand and looked deep into her eyes. "My beautiful darling, I must tell you everything."

Jack spoke of a lifetime of civil rights work. He told her of his desertion from the Marine Corps. He was a Ghandian pacifist. War was immoral.

Deirdre felt an overwhelming compassion for this man who had given up his freedom to stand up for his beliefs. She didn't know if she could be that courageous.

After twenty years of non-stop verbal abuse, Deirdre was enchanted with the concept of non-violence. His gentleness was a soothing balm to the abrasion created by those years. Jack talked in a hypnotic, near whisper, as though secrecy was imperative at all times. It made her feel exclusive.

When he finished, Deirdre's eyes were filled with tears and her heart and mind screamed in protest against those who had hurt this wonderful man. She would help him. His life would be better. She felt she had truly found her soul mate. The psychic was right.

JACK

When Deirdre first walked into the diner, Jack didn't pay much attention to her. She seemed to be in a bad mood, and obviously in a hurry. She demanded a menu, so Jack quipped that they didn't give those to customers.

She looked up at him in astonishment, and he winked, smiling at her with his eyes. In spite of her mood, he got a laugh out of her. Looking into her dark brown eyes, he recognized a familiar need. Her need was hunger. It was not food she was hungry for, though, but love. Looking her over, he realized she wasn't bad looking, and he could tell by her clothes and manner that she was doing okay financially. Most important, there was no ring on her left hand. Jack turned on the charm.

After she left, Jack asked one of the customers he'd seen talking to her where she worked. He learned her name was Deirdre Warren, and she was a Dean of one of the local colleges. He wasn't surprised. He could tell she was educated. Jack was pleased with his selection. Perhaps this one might actually be worthy of him.

When Deirdre came back again that evening, and again the next day, he knew he was reeling her in. Meeting her friends was a nice touch. They all seemed impressed with his humor. Women needed to feel special, Jack knew, so he talked only to her while the other women were around. They made a private connection with their eyes, shutting everyone else out. The eyes always got them.

Jack could give her what she craved, of that he was certain. His past sexual problem would not bother him with this one. He would make sure of that. This one would not turn him in.

The next day Jack called Deirdre at work and asked if she would come to the diner later that evening so that they could talk. She agreed.

Deirdre was so easy. She was a throwback to the sixties, a real bleeding heart. She bought his whole pacifism routine. Jack was intrigued by Deirdre's background in psychology. A fleeting, subliminal hope flashed through his mind as they spoke. *Maybe she could save him.* The next day he sent a huge bouquet of roses to her office with a card that read: TO THE STARS WITH LOVE.

Deirdre began driving him back to the halfway house each night and agreed to sponsor him. She would take him home on weekends. She arrived one evening with a small box wrapped as a gift. When he opened it, there was a key inside. She told him it was the key to her apartment. Jack smiled to himself. He knew he had her hooked.

DEIRDRE

It felt so good to be in love. Deirdre no longer wanted to keep her feelings private. She wanted to share her joy with all of her friends, but Deirdre's friends did not share her enchantment with Jack. She was disappointed by their reaction.

"He's been in prison," they reasoned. "People don't go to prison for protesting."

"I know," she told them. "I said the same thing, but there were special circumstances. Come on. You remember. A lot of people were arrested in the sixties."

Deirdre retaliated with stories of Thoreau and others who'd engaged in civil disobedience. Her college activist days had left her with numerous tales of injustice toward the innocent.

Most of them gave up when she, so adamantly, sprang to his defense. They appeared to be fearful for Deirdre. It was clear to Deirdre that there was something about Jack that they did not trust.

It was Mark, however, that finally revealed the truth. Mark had been Deirdre's friend for over fifteen years. They were like siblings. They shared each other's secrets, fears, loves, and desires. They helped each other through painful experiences.

Mark was not satisfied with Deirdre's explanation of Jack's incarceration. He went to the Prothonotary's office and researched Jack's arrest record. What he saw confirmed his fears. He phoned Deirdre and said that he needed to see her right away.

"What's the big urgency?" Deirdre asked, out of breath. "I rushed to get here."

"I thought you needed to see this," Mark answered, his face grim. He handed her the copy he made of Jack's record.

She didn't speak for a long time while she read of Jack's fraudulent activities. The record listed theft and fraud, and described money borrowed under false pretenses, mostly from women. "Well, it looks like I'm next on his list," she said at last.

"Deirdre—Mark began, but she cut him off.

"Don't. I can't talk about it now. I'll call you later."

Deirdre got into her car and drove to the diner. When she got there, she went to the counter. "Jack, I need to talk to you outside, now."

Jack had never seen Deirdre look so stern. He became instantly afraid. He asked someone to cover the counter and followed Deirdre outside.

When they reached the car, Deirdre thrust the papers at Jack. "Why me, Jack?"

Jack's hands began to shake as he read the report. He had to convince her to stay with him. "Please, Darling, let me explain. Its not the way it looks."

"Go to hell!" Deirdre took the papers out of his hand, got in the drove away. The phone was ringing when she walked in the door.

"Please, please. Just give me five minutes to explain," Jack pleaded. Deirdre hung up.

The next day, Deirdre called in sick to work. She hadn't taken a sick day in three years. This day, however, she just couldn't face anyone. What a fool she'd been.

Deirdre drove to the Rehoboth beach about two hours away. She walked on the boardwalk until she couldn't walk anymore. There were no answers there, only sadness. In moments she had lost her dream, her soul mate. She wasn't sure how she could face another day or how she could look her friends in the eyes. She got back in the car and drove home.

Once again, the phone was ringing when she walked in.

"I've been calling all day. I was so worried. They told me you were sick."

"Jack, leave me alone."

"Don't hang up. Please, just listen for one second. Let me talk to you face-to-face for just five minutes. That's all I ask. Five minutes and then I'll never bother you again."

Deirdre desperately needed to know why Jack had selected her. She felt so stupid, so vulnerable. Was she doomed to make bad choices in her romantic life? All of her insecurities became magnified in her mind.

"All right, Jack. Five minutes."

She waited in the parking lot outside of the diner. He came out within minutes of her arrival. He looked pale. His hands shook non-stop.

"Things aren't what they appear to be," he began haltingly. "You must understand. I would never hurt anyone. When Julie died, I fell apart. I was out of my mind. The only time I could stop thinking about her was when I was at the track. It's true that I borrowed money, but I paid a lot of it back. This money would have been paid back, too. Only I was arrested before I had a chance. That woman who turned me in, she was angry with me because I couldn't love her. I was honest with her from the very beginning. I told her I could never love anyone but Julie. But then I met you. I didn't believe it was possible to love two women with such intensity. I never dreamed I could find an even stronger love. Then I met you."

"Jack, you lied to me."

"No, darling. Everything of significance I told you was the truth. You can't believe everything in that report. Where do they say I went to school?"

"It says that you went to the University of Southern California."

"That's a lie. I went to school in Philadelphia. I can prove it. Here, here's my mother's phone number. Call her; talk to her. She'll tell you everything. I told you the truth about the Marines, about my civil rights work. She'll tell you the same."

Deirdre agreed to call Jack's mother. She needed to know the truth. Mrs. Stiles was warm and caring. Jack had told her how much he loved Deirdre. She said she had been afraid he would never find anyone after Julie. He was so upset when he lost her.

Deirdre was surprised. He must have been telling the truth about Julie, and he had told his mother about her. Maybe he did love her, after all, Deirdre thought.

Mrs. Stiles talked about what a wonderful child Jack was, how caring and thoughtful. "He was too sensitive to go into the Marines," she said. "He makes mistakes, but he doesn't mean to hurt anyone. He really needs someone like you. Someone who can be firm with him."

It didn't sound like the background of a sociopath as she'd begun to fear. Maybe things weren't as they appeared.

Nevertheless, Deirdre was hesitant about entering into another bad relationship. True, Jack was nothing like Hank, but he could have more serious problems.

She then consulted a psychiatric social worker. Together they reviewed Jack's history and the arrest record. The social worker agreed that Jack did not have the background of a sociopath.

"It sounds like he might be a pathological gambler, however," the social worker suggested.

"Of course," Deirdre agreed. "That would explain everything. He has an illness. He needs help."

"That doesn't mean you have to be the one to give it to him."

"Well, someone does. People have been turning their backs on him for years. He needs someone to truly believe in him and help him. He deserves a chance to prove himself."

The lines of a poem kept running through Deirdre's mind of *all the words of tongue and pen, the saddest are, it might have been.*

Deirdre forgave Jack. They were married three months after meeting in the Diner.

JACK

Jack knew Deirdre's friend, Mark, was trouble the minute he met him. He didn't expect the creep to actually copy his record, though. He was supposed to get home release this weekend. He longed to sleep in a real bed, without the animals making noises all night. Now this. What if she never forgave him?

Jack called his mother in a panic and warned her that Deirdre might be calling.

"Mom, I planned to tell her the truth eventually, but I wanted to give us time first. You understand, don't you?"

Mrs. Stiles sighed. "I suppose so Jacky. What do you want me to do?"

"Just talk to her when she calls, Mom. Tell her what a great son you have."

"You are a great son, Jacky. It would be nice if you found a girl to settle down with. I know you miss Julie."

Jack tensed at the sound of Julie's name. "Julie's dead, Mom, at least to me." "Okay, Jacky. If she calls, I'll talk to her. I love you, son."

Jack hung up the phone without further comment. He'd set the groundwork. Now he just had to get Deirdre to talk to him again. She refused last night, and today there wasn't any answer. Where could she be?

After about fifty attempts to reach Deirdre, she finally answered. He could tell she was tired. That was good; her resistance would be down. He was right. She gave in and agreed to meet him.

When she showed up at the diner she looked terrible, but less angry. He talked about fairness and honesty and second chances. As was his pattern, Jack began twisting reality to confuse her. Calling his mother, though, proved to be a stroke of genius. She agreed to make the call. When she left the diner that night, Jack felt better. Mom would fix it for him.

Deirdre seemed to soften after talking to his mom, but she kept asking questions about his background. The woman was really starting to get on his nerves. She might be more trouble than she was worth. If he didn't want to get out of that halfway house so bad, he might be tempted to drop her.

Thank God she finally came around. Gambling convinced her. Women are so stupid. They love to be needed. Deirdre had decided to save him from his gambling problem. Hah! That was a joke. Jack knew he had no such problem, but if that's what it took to get Deirdre to get him out of that hole, then so be it.

The first thing he was going to do as soon as he got that ring on her finger was to quit this dirty job and get some decent clothes. Life was definitely looking up again for Jack Stiles.

DEIRDRE

One of Deirdre's lifelong dreams was to complete her Ph.D. and start her own consulting business. While she had completed her comprehensive exams, she had never managed to write the dissertation that would give her the doctorate. Following her divorce, she'd experienced a depression that had left her too tired and unmotivated to care about her future. Instead, she'd filled her hours with hard, mind-numbing work.

Her marriage to Jack changed everything. He was the antithesis of Hank. Jack supported her education, and encouraged Deirdre to fulfill her dream.

"Darling, you're so smart. You've come so far. You can't give up now. You could never live with yourself if you didn't do this."

Deirdre felt renewed. For the first time in years, she had hope and purpose. The demands of her job, however, would never allow her to focus on a project with the intensity necessary to complete a dissertation. As risky as it was, she would have to quit work and concentrate. It might take months.

"I don't care if it takes every cent we have," he said. "You must do this."

Buoyed by Jack's emotional support and encouragement, Deirdre quit her job and began work on her dissertation. While she had struggled during her last marriage to complete her coursework without the emotional support of her husband, Jack provided a cheering section that lifted Deirdre's spirits and stimulated her energy. Jack read her literature review, suggested other articles and books, and offered praise for each progression. It was exactly the sort of encouragement she needed.

They estimated that this effort would require between three and six months, with at least another six months before they began to generate an income. She had enough savings to get them both through that period.

Jack had quit the diner immediately after they married. That job really wasn't right for him. They agreed that he should find something more suitable for his skills. In spite of his intelligence, however, Jack wasn't marketable. He hadn't really worked in any job of substance for more than a few months. He had tutored math and taught briefly at a school in Canada, but that wasn't enough to secure him a position of any merit.

They agreed that the best thing for him would be to wait until they began their enterprise and he would become a partner. Jack's role in this new endeavor was to be in marketing the business and keeping the books. With his gift for persuasion, he seemed the perfect choice for such a task.

The dissertation took six months. Deirdre did research at the library and worked on the computer during the day. Jack took care of their apartment. In the late afternoon, she would take a break and they would play tennis together. Jack lounged at the pool when she was writing.

They were together most of the time. He was loving and attentive. Deirdre anticipated that sex might be a problem for Jack. He had been in prison for three years. She was right. Jack found it very difficult to get an erection. When he did, intercourse lasted only a few seconds. Deirdre was patient with him. She loved him. Sex would get better later when Jack felt more confident. He had been through a lot.

Even though their sexual life was far from perfect, Jack was very romantic. He would bring home fresh flowers and small items that he thought would please her. He prepared gourmet meals and lighted candles for the dinner table. He told her frequently that he loved her.

It was, without question, the happiest six months of her entire life. And the most costly.

At some point during this period, Jack began to talk about going to the race- track. Since Deirdre had concluded that gambling had been Jack's downfall, she rejected the idea immediately. She told Jack that she did not want to discuss the racetrack until she finished her doctoral work; she needed to concentrate. He had agreed.

The day after she successfully defended her dissertation, Jack began to push to return to the track. Deirdre, however, was under the impression that, because he was still technically on probation, he would not be allowed to gamble. Not so. A visit to his probation officer determined that there was no such restriction. Jack told his probation officer and Deirdre that he wanted to go to the track to try to understand his past. Consequently, for Jack's birthday he requested, and received, a trip to the track. This was to be the beginning of their downfall.

JACK

Jack needed to go shopping. Deirdre agreed that he needed clothes. He loved shopping. He could spend hours picking out one sport coat; he would touch the fabric and try it on numerous times. Then, he would compare the price with other stores until he got the best one. Sometimes, he could convince the store to give him a lower price because it was on sale at another location. That was fun.

Deirdre seemed to enjoy shopping with Jack, and naturally he needed her to pay the bill. He needed a credit card so he didn't have to drag her around with him all the time. Deirdre agreed. She knew she couldn't be with him all the time.

Once given the green light, Jack started sending for cards from various banks in Deirdre's name. Just in case, he told her. He wasn't going to use them, he said, but it was good to have the credit if they needed it, especially since she wasn't working.

Deirdre balked at the number of cards, but he reasoned with her until she gave in. Jack had a way of making anything sound logical. After getting the credit cards, he then convinced Deirdre that he would manage the finances, pay bills, etc. while she focused her attention exclusively on her doctoral work. He wanted to feel needed, he told her, and Deirdre seemed touched by his consideration.

Shopping was fun, but Jack was starting to get bored. The apartment complex had a clubhouse with sauna and pool that kept him entertained for a few hours each morning, and he liked playing tennis when he could find a partner, but he missed the track.

When Jack raised the issue of returning to the track, Deirdre was less than pleased. Jack had the ability to talk nonstop when he wanted to persuade, and he raised philosophical issues, alluding to famous people who gambled. He talked about living each day to the fullest—Carpe Diem. She wouldn't budge, though. She said she needed to focus on her dissertation. He didn't see what difference that made, but realized he'd better wait.

As soon as Deirdre defended her dissertation and was granted her doctorate, Jack began pressuring her hard about the track. The hook that got her, however, was when he told her he wanted to research and write about his gambling experience. He could tell this idea really appealed to Deirdre. She believed that such research would aid in Jack's rehabilitation and growth. She also told him that his insight might benefit society. She was so easy.

Jack convinced Deirdre they could create a contract that would be a safeguard against disaster. He would keep a journal of wins and losses. He would begin with an agreed upon sum of money and would quit when it was gone. He would only attend the track when she could go with him, another safeguard. He would promise her anything to get back to the track. With his three years in prison, he'd been away far too long to suit him.

Deirdre bought his story hook line and sinker. The important thing was that Jack Stiles was back!

DEIRDRE

Deirdre was excited about their new experiment. This was going to be good for Jack, she was certain. She took journals with them to the track, followed his bets, and wrote about his reactions and those of the people around them.

Wanting to observe people in all areas of the track, they experimented with various sections, but Jack seemed to want to spend most of the time in the clubhouse area. Deirdre found the racetrack to be a fascinating resource for people watching. She was shocked at the number of people who spent their days betting on horses.

Many of the regulars were retired people, some couples, or small groups of men or women, but mostly men. The group members seemed to know each other by name and sat in the same areas. Most wore lucky garments, hats or sweaters. Often the garments were soiled or torn because the strength of the superstition would not allow them to part with the garment long enough to have it laundered.

Jerry, a retired plumber in his late sixties, always wore a red sweater. When he arrived wearing a blue sweater, Deirdre asked him what happened to the red one.

"Oh," he said, "my wife snuck it into the laundry and it's still wet."

The rest of the day Jerry blamed his losses on the missing sweater. The next day the red sweater was back.

"I told the old lady," Jerry announced to those nearby, "don't touch that sweater again. It don't need washing." The others nodded in agreement.

Arguments would break out when a newcomer took a seat normally frequented by a regular. Racing forms adorned the tables to protect sacred spots. It was considered bad manners to sit in a spot protected by a *form*.

Drinking and smoking were common among gamblers. There were two factions, those who did and those who had. The ex-smokers spoke loudly of their heart or lung surgery. Some carried oxygen. Non-alcoholic beer replaced what had once been the real thing.

Not all racetrack aficionados were retired persons, however. Men and women in dark suits (mostly men) dotted the tables—sometimes in groups, sometimes alone. Casual chats with the waitresses and snatches of overheard conversations revealed that most of those people were in sales or owned businesses.

Rainy days brought out contractors and seasonal workers. Inclement weather stimulated expectations for high wins. Many fancied themselves experts on *sloppy* track betting.

There was one group of lawyers who appeared every afternoon by three or four. Cheryl, their waitress, was a middle-aged woman who proclaimed she *never bet*. She told Deirdre that the group left work early nearly every day and bet large amounts of money.

"They mostly lose," she said. "Its funny. They're smart guys. They read the form, they know how to bet, but they love the long shots. They bet exactas and trifectas. You need to pick the first and second in an exacta and the first, second, and third in a trifecta. They bet impossible combinations. They don't seem to mind losing, though. Sometimes if they lose a lot, they don't tip me. They're all divorced." She shook her frizzled blond head in disgust. "I guess their wives couldn't take it."

Each bettor had a unique way of watching a race. Some were almost casual observers, as though it had no effect on them. These were usually the professional gamblers. They were calm and cool and kept their tickets covered. Others watched intensely, but kept quiet. They would reveal their wins or losses only through facial expressions, a grimace or a grin.

Then, there were the grumblers. They would yell and shout and curse. Often they threw the form or knocked over chairs when they lost. They tore up their tickets and threw them to the ground while blaming the track, the jockey, or the weather. Many gamblers would yell, cheer their horses in, groan when they lost, but quickly move on to the next race.

Almost all gamblers had idiosyncrasies. Tickets were kept in certain pockets or held in one hand. No one walked past during a race without risking the wrath of others. Betting habits ranged from offhanded guesses, the color or number of the horse, to computer programs which weighted jockey and horse records, track conditions, length of the race, etc.

While Deirdre was fascinated by her observations of the gambling culture, she soon became bored with the daily repetition. In addition, she began to worry about the frequency of their visits to the track. They were supposed to be starting a new business enterprise, but he showed no interest in the marketing plan Deirdre had developed. She had obtained mailing lists and asked him to mail out their brochures and follow-up with phone calls. He kept telling her he would, but always had an excuse why he didn't. He would do it next week, he had always said. He needed to organize the desk or to rearrange the office space. Deirdre was becoming anxious, and frustrated by Jack's lack of enthusiasm for their future.

Deirdre's frustration escalated to alarm when she walked into the betting area and discovered Jack tearing up losing tickets and throwing them on the floor. When she confronted him with the fact that they were supposed to be entered into the journal, he said the tickets weren't his. He had found them, and was checking to see if any were winners. Deirdre was not convinced.

Jack's mood began to change. He became restless and agitated when away from the track. He would get furious when he lost, throwing his racing form on the ground. In the evening, he spent all of his time and energies reviewing the racing form.

Late at night, Deirdre began to waken in a panic. She had always trusted her intuition. Since childhood, she would get a sense when something or someone was not right. She was usually on target. Something was not right, but she didn't know exactly what was amiss nor what to do about it.

After a particularly difficult night, she told Jack that she thought he should discontinue gambling for a while. Jack readily agreed, but then made excuses for continuing one more day, one more week.

With no help from Jack, Deirdre managed to obtain their first consulting contract. She was ecstatic. Being absent most days, however, Deirdre could no longer go to the track with Jack. They agreed that they would limit the racetrack to weekends.

In spite of his assurance that he would not go to the track without her, Deirdre would frequently call during the day and he wouldn't answer. Often, the phone would ring busy for hours.

She couldn't help but worry about where he was. Her anxiety prompted her to leave work early one day. When she arrived home he wasn't there. The phone was off the hook. By the time he walked in, two hours later, Deirdre was ready to explode. He claimed he had jogged to the store and had taken the phone off the hook so that if anyone called, they would call back. She accused Jack of lying.

The accusation prompted an intense response from Jack. He paced back and forth, breathing heavily, with an injured expression on his face. He spoke about his need for trust and honesty. He seemed so sincere. She began to feel guilty for not believing him.

The truth came out, however, when Jack's mother phoned Deirdre at work, something she'd never done before. She asked why Jack needed to borrow money from them. Deirdre thought they had over thirty thousand dollars in the bank, so she became confused and scared.

When she confronted Jack, he admitted that he had taken out all of their savings, and the bank account was empty. He had also run up credit cards to their limit, exceeding fifty thousand dollars.

Deirdre went to the bank to discover how this could have happened. The savings account, she believed, required both of their signatures to withdraw funds.

The account manager was nearly as upset as Deirdre when she reminded her of the last time the two of them came to the bank to withdraw money. At that time, Jack was informed that either of them could make a withdrawal. In her love dazed state Deirdre had paid little attention. She assumed that if she had not co-signed for a withdrawal, the money would still be there.

The worst, however, was the fact that Jack had begun to write bad checks, overdrawing their account. These checks could not be covered. Though they were completely broke, these checks would need to be paid. The insufficient checks included a check to the IRS, the rent check for the past two months, and several checks to local stores and businesses.

The world seemed to be spinning out of control. Deirdre felt incapable of controlling the downward spiral. As humiliating as it was, Deirdre agreed to borrow money from Jack's parents to pay the outstanding checks. The credit card debt was another issue. Deirdre researched all possibilities. She spoke to two attorneys, and took out books on bankruptcy. She consulted a credit counseling organization. There was no way she could repay all of the debt that Jack had incurred. Bankruptcy was the only solution. Her credit, which had always been impeccable, was now ruined. Her self-esteem destroyed.

Deirdre's state of shock quickly grew to rage. Why did Jack do this to her? She had given him a life, taken him from prison, and he had destroyed her.

"How could you do this?" she ranted at Jack. "What kind of a monster are you?" He merely looked back at her, shaking his head. In her rage, she threw a clock at him, hitting him on the side of the head. He looked at her in shock and hurt, but she felt no guilt at her display of violence. She began to actually visualize squeezing his neck until his head popped off. The image gave her some small pleasure.

Deirdre asked Jack to leave. "I want you out of here, now. I never want to see your lying face again. I was a fool to believe you would change."

Jack cried and begged and promised that he would do anything to make it up to her. "Please, Darling, don't give up on me," he begged. "I slipped, I know. I swear I'll never do it again."

He agreed to get a job to help pay back the money they borrowed to cover the bad checks. He swore he would never return to the track. He promised to go to Gambler's Anonymous.

As angry as she was, Deirdre couldn't throw him out in the street. There was no money to give him so he could get his own place. She felt trapped. It was like having a puppy that kept peeing on the floor. Only she couldn't give Jack to the SPCA. She was exhausted and had no energy to continue fighting with Jack.

Once again, Deirdre relented, telling herself that he had this one last chance and no more. He had learned his lesson and would never do this again. Another big mistake.

JACK

Jack was excited to be back at the track. It was even better now. He had money. He'd run to the ATM machine early in the morning while Deirdre was still asleep and take out cash advances. At first he only took a couple of hundred; after a while the withdrawals were more like a thousand. They would only let you take five hundred a day, so he had to use a couple of cards, but having money at the track was great.

Deirdre was no trouble. He would show her a few tickets and some winnings and let her keep her stupid journal. They would have long philosophical conversations at dinner about gambling and gamblers. That seemed to keep her happy.

He had to watch her, though. Sometimes she would wander around taking those dumb notes of hers. Once she caught him tearing up losing tickets. He was able to convince her that they weren't his, but after that he'd go to a different floor to place his bets, telling her he was going to the bathroom. She was so trusting; she believed anything he told her. No one goes to the bathroom that much.

After she got that contract, it was much better. As soon as she left for work, he would jump into his rental car and head for the track. If she called, he'd tell her he was jogging, or he'd leave the phone off the hook and tell her he was napping.

He'd had a bad streak of luck lately. Probably needed to increase his bets. Money was getting a little tight. After the credit cards all maxed out, he convinced that brain dead bank clerk to let him withdraw cash from Deirdre's savings account. He was her husband, after all. Now that money was gone as well. He'd long stopped trying to balance the checkbook, having written so many checks for cash he'd lost count. The bank started calling, saying they were overdrawn. Time to call Mom.

Dad took the call. Bad luck. He wanted to know why Jack needed money. Deirdre seemed to be doing okay financially. Why were they broke.

Not broke, Jack argued. They were having a cash flow problem. Some investments took up a lot of cash, and Deirdre wasn't working for a while. Now they had this new contract and the money would be rolling in soon. They just needed a few thousand. They'd pay it back next month. No problem.

Jack didn't count on his parents calling Deirdre. They'd become pretty close since the wedding, but he had no idea they'd tell her about the loan. He'd never seen her so mad. She actually threatened to throw him out. Jack started to panic.

He knew that Deirdre feared he had a gambling problem, so he used that to his advantage. Yes, he agreed, he was a compulsive gambler. He would get help.

He would go to Gambler's Anonymous. He would get a job to pay back his parents. Anything.

DEIRDRE

Jack and Deirdre agreed to go to G.A. together. She knew Jack was going under duress, but she didn't care. For her, it was a condition of their remaining together. For once in their relationship, Deirdre was adamant.

They both walked into the meeting with great apprehension. Deirdre had taken the lead and called the G.A. number in the phone book. A man, who only gave his first name, called her back. He gave Deirdre the dates and locations of the meetings. The one they decided to attend was the closest and the soonest.

There was a great deal of smoke. Everyone was drinking coffee. Deirdre learned later that many compulsive gamblers suffer from cross addiction, alcohol, drugs, etc.

The meeting began with the Serenity Prayer from St. Francis di Assisi, which served as the foundation for most 12-step programs: *God grant me the serenity to accept the things I can not change, the courage to change the things I can and the wisdom to know the difference.* The Serenity prayer was one of the 12-step experiences that Deirdre continued to use.

After the prayer, the members went around the table, introduced them- selves—first names only— and stated when they had placed their last bet. When Deirdre said that she was there for Jack, they asked her to wait outside the room. As it turned out, this was a closed meeting. It was only open to gamblers. Other meetings, open meetings, allowed family and friends to sit in.

They took a vote and said that she could not return, but that she could go to the Gamanon meeting being held next door. That meeting was for family members and close friends of gamblers. Deirdre reluctantly agreed.

The Gamanon meeting was predominately comprised of women. There was less smoke, but a lot of coffee. Everyone paid a small contribution each week for the coffee, but it was strictly voluntary. Some were so broke from their gambler's activities that they couldn't afford even a dollar a week.

This meeting also began with the serenity prayer, but after that it became mostly a review of their tales of horror. The one commonality was that they had all stayed with their gambler. They talked a great deal about forgiveness and letting go of the anger. Deirdre spoke of her rage, but they all assured her that it would pass. They did not agree with the bankruptcy; they said that was a mistake. Most of them had worked out slow payment plans; many had re-mortgaged their homes. Most were in debt for the rest of their lives.

They seemed to gain support from the shared pain in the group. Most of them had loved ones in the next room. Many of the couples had formed friendships and attended social activities together. Most had developed a dependency on the group, almost like another addiction.

Deirdre became more depressed as the weeks wore on. The anger continued, and she knew she didn't feel the same love for Jack. She felt trapped, however, and for some strange reason, felt responsible for Jack's recovery.

Most of the members spoke of gambling activities that were all consuming in their lives. They used bookmakers and gambled on everything from cards to football. They frequented casinos. It was a twenty-four hour activity.

Jack's gambling activity had been very different from what was being described in these meetings. Since he discovered the racetrack, horse racing had been his primary focus. He never gambled on anything but the horses, never even bought a lottery ticket. Deirdre found the discrepancy confusing. Did this mean that he wasn't really a pathological gambler?

Jack took advantage of her confusion to convince Deirdre that he was not a compulsive gambler after all. He acknowledged that he did have a problem with money. He obviously hadn't been able to handle money. He suggested that she made a mistake in allowing him to manage their finances. He further said that he'd been so ashamed about mismanaging their money; he was trying to recoup it by winning at the track.

Jack's logic, when looked at objectively, was convoluted, empty and ludicrous. Deirdre wanted to believe that her husband never intentionally put them in this devastating position. As usual, she was too tired to reason logically, and was more than eager to discontinue the depressing weekly activity that was wearing her down.

The G.A. and Gamanon experience was designed to be a support group run by its members and not a therapy group. But the one belief that Deirdre took away from that experience is that a trained professional might have been able to guide the group more productively and avoid some of the pitfalls. For example, some members were allowed to dominate the discussion and would go on for the entire meeting about personal issues.

The group was quick to give advice such as forgive and forget. Deirdre was struggling with her own conscience because of her anger toward Jack.

After Jack and Deirdre abandoned G.A., they discussed developing a treatment plan for gamblers which was short of abstinence, and did not involve a support group. Deirdre expressed her belief that continuing any addictive activity merely served to reinforce the addiction. Smoking clinics used the term *you are only a puff away from a pack a day*.

After many long discussions, Jack convinced Deirdre that they would be doing a service by developing an alternative treatment plan. Most important, Deirdre believed that working to help others would provide Jack with the necessary motivation for his own recovery.

Jack and Deirdre went to training for certification to treat compulsive gamblers. Jack began to read voraciously, not only about gambling treatment, but anything related to psychology or psychotherapy. They began to attend other workshops and seminars in all areas of counseling and treatment techniques. Jack became obsessed with the concept of becoming a therapist. He wanted to go to school.

Deirdre was delighted with the idea of Jack's returning to school and with his enthusiasm. Jack took a certification program in couples communication, and began to work with Deirdre on counseling couples in communication conflicts. The blend of Deirdre's skills and Jack's charisma was extremely effective. Couples loved the treatment they received. They most of all loved Jack. He seemed effective and brilliant. All of his reading and seminar work had paid off.

Deirdre began to feel that her love for Jack was truly fated. This was the work they were meant to do together. He was her soul mate. On their anniversary, Deirdre wrote to Jack:

> We are truly soul mates, you and I.
> Often unalike, we vie for truth
> In frequent confrontation.
> Leaving each assault a cleansed spirit.
> As sand and sea, sun and earth,
> We vary in hues and pulsing rhythms.
> At once child and parent, sibling and lover,
> Antagonist and friend.
> Parched in our aloneness, we inspire
> Like the desert flower.
> Alive in those who see in us
> To be forever
> Soul Mates

At the end of that year, however, Jack had still not found an educational program that suited him. He didn't want to go to the local university. He had become so enmeshed in the work that he was doing and his reading that he opted for a nontraditional program.

Deirdre somehow managed to scrape up five thousand dollars to pay for Jack to begin his studies in counseling psychology through a program in Idaho. The design was that he would read and do assigned projects, write papers and take open-book exams. Deirdre had never thought much of such programs, but Jack seemed happy and that made Deirdre happy. Most of all Jack seemed to be productive for the first time in his life. In her worst nightmares, Deirdre couldn't image the damage Jack could do with such power, and she never came close to suspecting the nature and severity of his perpetration. Such violation seemed beyond comprehension!

JACK

Jack had found his true calling. Of all his personas, this was without question the best yet. He was now a *psychotherapist*. He loved it. Carrying textbooks into restaurants, he would flaunt his new identity, offering advice to the wait staff about relationships and life. People started calling him Doc. This was better than the other identities he had used, because now he had Deirdre to help him. Being with her legitimized him, gave him credibility.

Naturally, he never actually called himself a doctor in front of Deirdre, she would be furious. She was such a pain about some ethics manual she kept shoving at him to read. Who cared what those tight assed people thought? If someone referred to him as Doc, he would just tell her they were confused, thinking it was he that was the Ph.D.

Deirdre always referred to herself as a counselor. That sounded so mundane. Psychotherapist was much more impressive. Most assumed he was a psychiatrist, and he never corrected them.

Going to those boring seminars was just a way to appease Deirdre in the beginning. But then, Jack started to realize what a great opportunity this could be for him.

What power! There was no end to the possibilities this opened up. He needed to get some sort of degree, though. He knew Deirdre would love it if he went back to school, but that was definitely out of the question. Who needed to sit in class all day listening to some jerk? He had better things to do. He would get one of those degrees through the mail. It didn't matter, anyway. Jack knew more than any of those pompous professors. After the third seminar, he was sure he could handle this career with no problem.

Now and then Deirdre would bug him about his progress in the program, but he would put her off. As long as she believed he was working on a degree, she left him alone.

Jack's first big opening came when Deirdre signed them up for a couple's communication training. The weeklong seminar provided a certificate as a couple's communication specialist. That certificate became his entry into the field of psychotherapy.

Deirdre agreed to allow him to work with her as a paraprofessional. She explained to the couples that came to see them that she was the counselor and he was a communication specialist.

Jack worked side-by-side with Deirdre and quickly discovered that he could. use many of his techniques with women to develop trust with the clients. They loved him. While Deirdre counseled in casual pants and sweaters, Jack always wore designer suits, dress shirts, and ties. The clients were impressed with him, and quickly gave him their trust. He seemed so genuine and caring, that even Deirdre was impressed.

"You have a true gift for counseling, Jack. I knew you were a good person; you just needed the right direction."

After a few months, though, Jack tired of having Deirdre watching his every move and critiquing him following each session. It was time for a change.

Deirdre worked on her consulting contract during the day, so Jack took all the incoming calls and scheduled new appointments. It was easy for him to schedule appointments during the day, with him alone. Naturally, he never mentioned these sessions to Deirdre.

He would tell the clients he needed to be paid in cash, and they complied. Jack was so convincing that he could easily talk them into anything. Even the educated professionals were taken in by his assured manner and vocabulary. They believed this man knew what he was doing. He didn't bother to inform them of his credentials, or lack thereof, and they assumed he was a psychotherapist with the highest credentials. Jack was amused that they never asked to see his documentation.

With the cash he was getting from clients, Jack soon amassed a stash of money to enable him to return to the track. His pattern became to counsel in the morning, go to the track in the afternoon, and return home before Deirdre arrived that evening. She was so tired most of the time, when he said there hadn't been any new clients, she seemed relieved. He would schedule a few for the two of them now and then, but quickly switch them to him alone by calling them and telling them she was no longer available and he would need to see them during the day. Deirdre never suspected. She was so easy.

Several months into Jack's new pattern, he started losing heavily at the track. He needed a new source of income. An idea began to form in Jack's mind. The clients were so trusting, and they all seemed to have money to spare, why not start a little investment business?

Jack's first victim was a surgeon. George and his wife had seen Deirdre and him for counseling prior to their separation. When Jack started seeing him alone, George confessed he'd been hiding some funds from his wife until the settlement was final. This proved to be the perfect opportunity for Jack to start his new investment program.

Jack informed George that he had a secret investor who could get him a forty percent return on his investment within a couple of months. He had said that he guaranteed the investment and that there was nothing illegal about it (no drugs or syndicate involvement). George eagerly handed Jack twenty-six thousand dollars in cash the next day. The two men agreed that there could be no receipt or paper trail. Deirdre wasn't to be told, nor would Jack provide George with the name of the investor.

Jack began to try out his investment opportunity with other clients. Some were less enthusiastic, but most jumped at the idea. Only a few commented that the arrangement seemed a bit unethical. Those people soon stopped coming to see him. He didn't care about them. There were enough investors to keep him going for a long time.

The big flaw in Jack's scheme was that he never paid any of them back. They began to call and hound him for their money, leaving long messages if he didn't answer the phone. In fear that Deirdre would hear one of them, he changed their voicemail to one that required a code in order to play back messages. Jack kept changing the code so that Deirdre couldn't check the messages. She stopped trying altogether.

One Saturday evening they had just returned from a late movie and one of the clients was waiting at the front door. Jack was furious. He told Deirdre he would talk to him alone. She agreed, but he could tell she didn't like it. Jack told the man if he ever came to his home he would never see his money again. The man left, but swore he would be back. Jack told Deirdre the man had met him a long time ago at the track and wanted to borrow some money.

On another occasion, Deirdre came home early and one of the clients that they had formerly seen together was there talking to Jack. She said hello to the client and asked Jack to step into the other room. Jack knew that Deirdre would never start a confrontation in front of a client, but he was going to need an explanation.

"Why is he here, Jack?"

"Oh, he just stopped in to thank us for helping him. He and his wife just got back together. He was a little embarrassed and wanted to talk to me alone." "Why would he want to talk to you alone?"

"It's a guy thing, sweetheart. I promised him I would keep his confidence. Surely you understand."

Deirdre nodded, but he could tell she didn't understand and didn't like it. The client left immediately. Jack told him she had a crisis to deal with and he needed to end the session.

Close calls were occurring more and more often, but Jack found the danger exciting. He loved seeing just how close he could come to discovery and still manage to keep his secret. Nevertheless, he started thinking he might need to disappear before long.

Jack read in the paper about a lawsuit started by some guy who developed a rare form of lung cancer related to asbestosis called mesothelioma. He started telling the clients that he had been diagnosed with the disease and was going to have to stop counseling soon. He needed a little time to get their money back. Most of them backed off for a while after that, and some even gave him a loan to help out with the medical bills.

He knew not all of them were convinced, though, and was afraid they might actually go to the police, or to Deirdre. They'd just moved into a new house, and he hated to leave it and his new career, but time was definitely running out.

He'd dumped most of his cash at the track the day before and needed some money to get away. He had a couple of winning tickets in his pocket, though, and decided to make one last try at the track before he took off.

Jack Stiles was arrested that afternoon as he entered the racetrack.

DEIRDRE

Sometime around four in the morning, following Jack's arrest, Deirdre had finally fallen asleep. Her pillow was stained with a combination of make-up and tears. Her eyes were swollen and sore, and the ache in her chest would not ease its grip.

The ringing in her head refused to go away. Swimming upward from a familiar dream in which she was running from some faceless creature, she realized the noise was her phone. Through her sleep-fogged vision, she could see the clock. It was not quite six.

This was to be the first of many calls that day. Most of them asked for Jack. *Where was he? When would he be back?* The sheer number of calls was astonishing. It was after ten that evening before the calls finally stopped coming.

Jack had always taken the calls when she was at work. When she came home, Jack would switch them to the voicemail, saying this was their private time together.

Two days following Jack's arrest, Deirdre picked up the morning paper to see her husband's picture staring up at her.

COUPLES BROUGHT HIM THEIR TROUBLES AND GOT CONNED.

Deirdre couldn't stop shaking as she read of the horrors that had been perpetrated by her *soul mate*. She had let all of those people down. How could she possibly have exposed them to this monster?

What kind of a therapist was she? The article continued to talk about Dr. Warren, suggesting that she was his willing accomplice.

After the article appeared, the nature of the calls changed. The first one came around 8:30 in the morning. "Is it true?" a familiar voice asked.

Charles and his wife had been one of Deirdre and Jack's first clients. Deirdre believed she and Jack had helped the couple.

"You saw the article?"

"Is it true?" Charles repeated.

"Charles, Jack has been arrested for fraud." Her face burned with humiliation. Deirdre felt she would choke on the question, but she had to ask it. "Charles, did you ever give Jack money to invest?"

The silence that returned her question was all of the answer she needed. "Charles?"

"Are you trying to tell me you didn't know?" Charles snarled.

Deirdre couldn't believe she was having this conversation. "I am so very sorry, so sorry," she repeated. The drumming in her head was so loud; it seemed impossible to make her brain work.

"Please, Charles, tell me what happened?"

"I can't talk to you anymore." The voice seemed far away. He hung up.

The phone rang all day. Each time the ringing began, Deirdre wished she could ignore it, turn it off, or rip it from the wall, but guilt forced her to confront each caller no matter how hostile. The stories began to run together.

"Jack told me he had a wonderful investment opportunity for me." John, an engineer who had seen Jack and Deirdre to learn how to communicate with his wife without fixing the problem, told Deirdre that Jack had said he could get him a forty percent return on his money in sixty days.

"I gave him ten thousand dollars. The sixty days was up over a month ago. I asked Jack about the money, and he said that the investment was a little behind schedule but I would get the money. I haven't been able to get him on the phone for two weeks."

"He told me he had lung cancer and was going to have surgery," revealed a former client that Jack and Deirdre had counseled together. "Jack had done so much for me and my wife. We wouldn't be together if it weren't for him. When he asked for some money, he said it was for life insurance to protect you in case he died. I couldn't turn him down."

Some of the calls came from people she had never met, others from ones she knew well, people she had counseled. "How could you not know?" They asked. She knew they felt betrayed, and felt she had betrayed them.

A few seemed to understand. Some seemed sorry for her. "You must be devastated." The caller and her husband had been working on communication skills with Deirdre and Jack. Jack had started seeing them without her, telling Deirdre they had decided they no longer needed counseling. Her husband had given Jack four thousand dollars, but she had questioned the offer.

"I told Jack it seemed a little too good to be true. I didn't know Mark had given him the money until this morning. When he read the article he said, *Poor Jack.* I said, *Poor Deirdre.*"

Many of the callers were hostile and threatened Deirdre. "I want my money back, bitch. Don't try to tell me you didn't know what he was doing. I'll take you to court if I have to."

"I would lock my doors if I were you," another caller said.

A young woman called. She hadn't been a client, but had worked as a bartender in a restaurant Jack frequented. She had not seen the article, but wanted to know where Jack was. Deirdre told her. The woman began to cry.

"That money was everything I had," she sobbed. "He knew I was having trouble getting a house for my kids. I told him my husband left and I only had a few thousand dollars, not enough for a house. Jack said he could double my money in sixty days. The time has been up for weeks. I've tried to contact him, but he never returns my calls."

"Why didn't t you mention this to me?" Deirdre asked. "We've been in the restaurant several times in the past few weeks."

"Jack made me promise not to say anything. When I tried to talk to him in the restaurant, he said he would call me. But he never did. Oh, God!" She hung up.

"How could he do this to them? To me?" Deirdre wailed. It was then that she knew for certain this was no mistake. Jack did these horrible things. Deirdre felt sick with grief. What had he done with all that money?

"How could you do this?" She asked Jack that night when he called to insist she bail him out.

Jack kept repeating, "I can beat this thing. Just get me out." Deirdre didn't know what Jack meant by *beat this thing*, but she wanted to know what he did with all that money.

At first he wouldn't answer her, but eventually he said in a barely audible voice, "There is no money. It's gone."

Deirdre didn't have to ask where. She knew the clients' money the had gone to the racetrack.

The next evening there was a knock at the door. When Deirdre opened the door a man who said Jack had counseled him demanded to come in. He was the same man she had seen outside their door, the one Jack had told her wanted to borrow money.

Deirdre stood aside and allowed him to walk into the living room. He was obviously angry. He waived a promissory note in her face.

"If you don't want to go to jail with that lying husband of yours, you'll sign this." The note said that Deirdre would pay him a sum of twenty thousand dollars over a period of eight months.

Deirdre was astonished. She was feeling such shame that she might have agreed to anything, but the numbers were beginning to add up. She didn't have that kind of money. "I can't pay you this. I don't even know if I can afford to continue living here."

"You need to cooperate with me," he said in a threatening tone. "I can tell those investigators that you were in on this deal. They'll arrest you, too."

Deirdre finally began to get angry. "I suggest you tell the investigators anything and everything you know. I intend to do the same. Now I'm going to have to ask you to leave." She walked to the front door and opened it.

"I hope you have life insurance," he growled as he slammed the door behind him.

The next day a notice appeared on Deirdre's door. The flyer had been circulated in her neighborhood. The notice called her a criminal and demanded her arrest. It read:

BEWARE! THERE IS A CRIMINAL IN YOUR NEIGHBORHOOD!

We will not rest until Dr. Deirdre Warren is in prison with her husband.

This is a public service message. Please use caution until Dr. Warren is locked up with her husband. Look for updates in the paper.

The notice gave her address, license number and make of her car. Anger was a safer emotion than the devastating depression she'd been feeling. In fury, Deirdre called an attorney. The woman listened politely, but informed Deirdre they could do nothing unless they knew who put the notice on the door. The notice never appeared again, but Deirdre looked at her neighbors and wondered which one circulated the notice.

Why? Deirdre asked herself over and over again. She needed answers, and had an idea where they might be found. Jack had kept a box full of his former wife's diaries. He said that she had died ten years before Deirdre and he had met. Jack said he had loved his wife Julie desperately and couldn't bear to part with the diaries.

Once, a few years after they were married, Deirdre had asked to read the diaries. I want to know the woman you loved so much, Deirdre had told Jack. I think that reading the diaries will be like sharing your past. I want to get inside of you, to feel closer to you.

Jack's face had closed into an angry mask. *Those diaries are personal. They belonged to a beautiful, innocent woman. She left them in my trust. How can you ask me to betray that trust? She wrote those words in a private expression of love. She did not mean them to be read by a curious and jealous stranger. I can never violate her memory in such an unforgivable manner.*

Deirdre had never asked about the Diaries again. But Jack wasn't there now, and she needed answers.

She took out the box and opened the first diary at 6:00 on Friday evening. The first journal covered Jack and Julie's third year together. There were no diaries for the first two years. Deirdre looked at the last one and knew right away that she had to read them all.

Deirdre read until her eyes began to blur. Her sleep was filled with Julie's words. The next morning, coffee in hand, she returned to the diaries. There were some pictures of Julie amidst the diaries. Deirdre could see Julie's face as she read of her hopes, fears, and desperation. The woman began to take on a physical, living dimension in Deirdre's mind. She felt Julie was communicating with her. The words were a warning. A shiver ran up her body as the coffee chilled, unnoticed in the cup.

Why did you write these? Deirdre wondered. There was an entry for almost every day of Julie's life with Jack Stiles over a period of nearly seven years. In the last book, Deirdre found what she had been looking for. Julie was not dead. She had left Jack, had run away in desperation after nine years. She must have fled so quickly she left everything behind, including the diaries. Her farewell letter to Jack was stuck in the last few pages of the final diary.

By Sunday night, Deirdre felt she knew Julie intimately through those diaries. Her emotions during that weekend had ranged from shock, to laughter, to sadness. When she closed the last book, she knew what she had to do.

The next morning Deirdre called the Attorney General's Office and asked to make an official statement. She took the diaries with her.

Deirdre had a good friend who worked as a social worker in the criminal justice system.

"Be careful when you talk to them," her friend had cautioned. "They're not your friends." The words echoed through Deirdre's mind as she gave her statement.

When she arrived, the investigator, a man in his early fifties who called himself Frank, looked grim but kind. Throughout the entire experience, she felt he was trying to tell her something.

"You realize that anything you turn over to us can be used against you," he warned.

"You need to see these," Deirdre answered. "I need to help. I have to do something." She could feel the tears threatening to spill from her eyes, and swallowed hard to force them back.

Frank nodded without speaking. He reached over and turned on a tape recorder after asking her permission.

The statement took three hours. The worst moment was when they read her her rights. The words *you have the right to remain silent* never seemed as menacing to her as they did on that day. She began to shake out of control, and her stomach formed a tight knot that spread into her chest, making breathing difficult.

Were they going to arrest her? Thoughts of jail flashed through Deirdre's mind frequently during her discussion with Frank. What if they didn't believe her? What if they thought she knew about and even aided Jack in his schemes?

Deirdre knew she couldn't provide bail for Jack. She couldn't bring herself to support him, legally or otherwise. She vowed Jack Stiles would never be allowed to hurt anyone again.

The warning look that Jack had given her in the courtroom following his arraignment kept flashing in Deirdre's mind. Shaking off the fear, she told herself he couldn't hurt her from prison.

In spite of her constant exhaustion and lack of sleep, Deirdre had no choice, but to return to work; she needed the money. Jack had neglected to pay most of their bills, although she had given him the money to do so. The hypnotic television, which had been her escape, suddenly stopped working. Thinking there was a problem with the cable, she called to discover it had been shut off for lack of payment. The paper stopped coming as well. Same reason. Phone calls revealed their American Express bill was four thousand dollars. How could he have gam- bled away all that money? If he hadn't gambled it away, what had he done with it?

Walking into work, Deirdre was certain she would lose her morning coffee. How could she face the people who had respected her for so many years? Would they believe she belonged in prison with him?

Forcing herself through the front door, she walked quickly toward her office. Most of her colleagues avoided eye contact. Others gave her a look she began to call the *leprosy* look, as though she had some fatal and contagious disease. Fortunately, few of her co-workers thought she was involved in Jack's schemes, but she overheard many asking each other, "How could she be so stupid?"

FRANK

Frank shook his head sadly as Deirdre left his office. Erin Shanahan, the deputy attorney general assigned to the case, entered abruptly through a side door.

"She knows more than she's letting on."

"Erin, she's telling the truth. I talked to the arresting officers. Her husband had files hidden under the mattress, for Christ sakes. Why would he do that, if she knew what he was doing? Hell, she's his worst victim. At least the others have us on their side. She doesn't have a clue what she's up against."

"Well, you can feel sorry for her if you want to, Frank, but if I find one piece of information I can use against her, she's toast."

"I think you're more interested in getting your name in the paper."

"Hmm, well this guy's going down hard. And if she had any part in it, she's going with him. You can't be married to someone for seven years and not know what he's up to."

"Erin, listen to her testimony. She thought she was rehabing him. Damn!" He shook his head. "She's obviously a bright lady. How can some women be so dumb when it comes to men?"

"Well, I'm going through every file. If nothing else, we can go after her license.

Let's notify all the victims. I'm sure we can get some of them to file a complaint against her."

"No question about that. I think a couple of em would lynch her if they could get away with it."

"Can't blame them for that. God, what a violation! Can you imagine going to a therapist for help, and getting scammed out of your life savings?"

Erin started to leave the office, then turned. "So, why do you think she brought in those diaries? They certainly prove he had a criminal history."

"Yeah, they do. I think she believes she's helping us."

"But why? Maybe she thinks we'll go easy on her."

"No, I actually think she believes she's doing the right thing."

"You're getting too soft, Frank. Maybe you should think about retiring."

Frank watched Erin walk away. Leaning back in his chair, he reviewed his notes one more time, thinking about what Erin had just said. He shook his head. There was no question in his mind. Dr. Deirdre Warren had been completely taken in by Jack Stiles. She wasn't the first, though. As far as he could tell, living off of smart women had been a way of life for this guy. Frank felt a mixture of disgust and admiration. How did he do it? How did one man get such power?

DEIRDRE

Deirdre was astonished by the slowness of the justice system. The first few weeks were a bizarre mixture of numbness and pain as Deirdre uncovered more of Jack's lies and violations. She had been married to a man she never knew. Thinking about their lives together was so painful, she forced herself to focus on responding to all the calls from Jack's victims, and providing as much information as possible to the Attorney General's Office. In addition, she began divorce proceedings. There was some small relief in knowing that he would no longer be her husband. If only she'd left him sooner. If only....

When the calls began to dwindle, Deirdre was left staring at her own dismal future. Wandering from room to room in zombie-like motion, she was unable to focus on anything for more than a few minutes. Flipping the channel button on the remote, but not stopping long to watch anything, she picked up a book and stared at the same page for several moments before giving up. Feelings of guilt and shame had immobilized her. She kept asking herself why? Why did she allow this to happen? Why didn't she end the marriage sooner? Why did she marry him in the first place? There were no easy answers, only more questions.

In the middle of the night, when she couldn't sleep, Deirdre kept remembering the red flags, and the times that she should have left Jack. A few months before he was arrested, Deirdre had confided to a colleague that she feared the marriage was a mistake.

"I just wish he would leave," she'd admitted. "I know he won't, though. Why should he? I've given him a cushy life. I know that if I tried to leave, he would just follow me. I'm so tired of trying to second-guess him. I don't think I have the energy for that kind of struggle. How could I let myself get into such a mess?"

The woman listened sympathetically, but there didn't seem to be any words of wisdom to solve the problem. Most of her friends had long since tired of Deirdre's patience with Jack. They were no longer there to offer support. Deirdre had felt very alone, and very trapped.

She also remembered the lies. He had run up a large credit card bill. She had written a check to pay it, but Jack offered to drop it in the mailbox. Some sixth sense forced her to call to check on the balance. They had never received the check. Knowing she had already deducted the money from the checking account, he threw the check away and wrote a counter check for the cash. In addition, he had been intercepting the bills. Deirdre discovered that particular deceit the very day before his arrest.

The therapy sessions with Kathy Ruscko, a psychologist, increased Deirdre's anxiety.

"You seem angry. Do you know with whom you are angry?"

"I'm not sure. I guess, at times with myself. Why was I so weak?"

"Do you see yourself as weak?"

"I didn't think so, but I must be."

"You must be?"

Deirdre laughed, "I hate it when you counsel me."

"I'm only following your own train of thought. You must be weak?"

"Okay, okay. If I weren't weak, then why did I allow Jack to do what he did?"

"Is it possible that he was providing something for you that had been missing?"

Deirdre shook her head. She didn't want to think about how lonely she had been feeling when she'd first met Jack. Yes, he had filled a void for her, but that was no excuse. The sessions were painful, and elicited more questions.

It was only at work that Deirdre felt able to focus, forgetting all those questions for brief periods of time. She clamped desperately onto her professional demeanor during those daytime hours. Several times during the day, however, reality would resurface and she felt she might collapse at any moment. Running into the bathroom, she took deep gulps of air and fought back the tears until she felt in control.

On those days when she was able to feel more than an empty throbbing, she sobbed to and from work and most of the evening. Sleep was close to impossible. Sleeping only in brief, two-hour increments, she would wake in a panic, with tears soaking her pillow.

Deirdre was exhausted most of the time. Her head ached constantly and she had ongoing stomach cramps. Her psychologist had recommended that she get a prescription for an anti-depressant, Zoloft.

"I couldn't." Deirdre shook her head. "I've never taken anything stronger than an antihistamine before."

Kathy smiled. "Try it, Deirdre. It might help."

She was hesitant, but desperate. For Deirdre, the Zoloft was magic. She didn't feel euphoric by any means, but did feel nearly human. She felt that she could. function. Unfortunately it intensified the already existing stomach cramps. Every twenty minutes or so her stomach would remind her of its painful existence.

After a few weeks, however, Deirdre's emotions became so flat that she couldn't experience any feeling, good or bad. Even though Kathy repeatedly assured her that she must forgive herself for Jack's actions, Deirdre still felt she needed to be punished. As illogical as it seemed, the emotional pain was her punishment. Deirdre stopped taking the pills. The pain returned in full force, but the short-term use seemed to have enabled her to re-group enough to function. Knowing that she could return to it if it got unbearable helped a great deal.

Deirdre stared in disgust at her treadmill. The energy it took to climb on and work off those extra pounds just wasn't there. Instead, she chose to hang her towels on it. Who cared how she looked? When she could focus on television, she watched hours of mindless sitcoms while eating boxes of chocolate. Watching Love Boat reruns, one evening, she ate a box of left over cookies and a bag of chocolate covered peanuts. Discovering the joy of Ben and Jerry's *Cherry Garcia* ice cream, she kept thinking she could lose weight later. Much later.

It would be so easy to give up, to just go to sleep and never wake up. Going to work was so painful. Each day she had to walk through that door and see those leprosy looks, some in pity, some in disgust, it became more and more difficult. Her pride was demolished. She lacked the conviction to convey her opinions with any authority, making her supervisory sessions ineffectual.

Nevertheless, she had to go to work. Her sense of responsibility overcame her desire to escape. For example, her cat, Pax, kept reminding Deirdre of her needs. So, she needed to shop—for cat food at least. Going naked to work was not an option. The laundry had to be done. Finally, what pride she had left forced her to pay as many of the bills as her dwindling bank account permitted.

Socializing was nearly as painful as the work environment. Well-meaning friends often asked Deirdre out to social events. Small gatherings of two or three close friends were comforting and precious. She felt cocooned in their support and acceptance. Anything larger or more formidable, however, created a desire in her to run screaming from the room.

One evening after work, Deirdre was talked into attending happy hour with a friend. The experience appeared harmless enough until some stranger came to the table and sat down with them. He began to make small talk as though sitting with them was perfectly acceptable. Her friend smiled and laughed. Deirdre began to feel unreal, as though she was watching them but wasn't there. A fire siren clanged danger in her head. The man may have been very nice and harmless enough, but to Deirdre he represented the unknown and unwelcome. She left immediately, determined to forgo happy hours in the future.

In spite of her efforts, the bills piled up. Deirdre's house was more than she could afford but the very thought of moving was completely overwhelming. She looked around at all the books that would need boxing, and thought of all the decisions that would need to be made.

No, she couldn't bring herself to make any major decisions, or many minor ones.

The press continued to find reasons to write about Jack and her involvement with him. On numerous occasions, she picked up the paper to find her picture staring back at her. At first, she didn't recognize herself. This person they wrote about was not her. Yet, the article used her name and her picture. Where did they get this information? How could they twist the facts like this?

Walking into work knowing everyone had seen the article, felt like appearing naked to take her finals. Unprepared. Someone always managed to copy the article and leave it on her desk, just in case she had been spared the pleasure. A letter to the Editor demanded to know why she wasn't in jail with her husband.

Due to the negative publicity, her job was threatened. A colleague showed her an E-mail sent to her supervisor by a higher-level administrator. The message demanded to know why Deirdre was still working there. He insisted that her contract be cancelled. While her immediate supervisor was supportive, there were many who agreed her contract be eliminated. For three months, she didn't know if she would be employed another day. Finally, she was informed that her contract would not be renewed.

Consequently, she was forced to apply for jobs, which was stressful for most people under normal circumstances. For Deirdre it was agony. During the interviews they always wanted to know about her husband and the newspaper articles. Often, copies of the articles would be on their desks. The looks on their faces told her they either didn't believe her or thought she must be very stupid.

One interviewer asked how he could possibly hire her. He waved one of the articles in her face. "You have no credibility."

She didn't get the job.

The intense social phobia did constant battle with the aching loneliness. Hungry to be near other humans without the need to interact, she wandered the mall, watching the smiling people, listening to the laughter. Memories of shopping with Jack flooded her mind. Jack had loved clothes. He would touch the fabric, trying on clothes for hours before selecting that one, perfect item. His hands would shake with excitement. How could she miss him so deeply? She forced herself to remember his violations to replace the pain with anger.

Movies also brought painful thoughts of fun times with Jack. He knew every line in *Casablanca* as well as most classic movies. These movies were now spoiled for Deirdre. She was unable to watch for more than a few moments before sobbing. Why did he have to destroy their lives?

As lonely as she was, Deirdre couldn't begin to think about a personal life. An old friend introduced her to a kind and attractive man. They went out to dinner on several occasions, and once to the theatre. Deirdre realized that he was eager to develop the relationship. She felt she had nothing to give. How could she enter into a relationship when she didn't exist?

A few hours before they were to leave for a planned evening out, she called him.

"I'm just not ready," she said. "I hope you can forgive me."

"Goodbye Deirdre," he said quietly.

Small pockets of support kept her going. Her two office mates helped her cope with the stares and whispers. They allowed her to vent daily, giving her space when she needed it and constant encouragement. They never once questioned her innocence or involvement in Jack's schemes.

In addition, a few wonderful friends and colleagues helped her to believe in humanity. These dear friends brought her dinner once a week. They sat and talked and joked and described horrible things they could do to Jack. It was healing. It was a balm to her psyche. Deirdre would be forever grateful to them.

In the midst of the worst wave of hostile phone messages, there was one message that said, "Hi, this is Dan—a friend." That brief message gave her hope and brought forth a flood of tears. Thank you, she said to the phone. Thank you, Dan.

The most meaningful support came from a small, but very significant source. Deirdre's cat, Pax, was always there when she returned home. With an intuitive sense, Pax would curl onto her lap and offer her furry warmth and comfort. When there were moments, fleeting thoughts, that she could not survive, Pax reminded her that she was needed.

Not all friends were supportive, however. Some of them judged, and judged harshly. Many repeated the litany, "I told you not to get involved with him. You should have known better. You allowed him to hurt those people." It seemed at times that Deirdre's biggest mistake was not heeding her friends' advice.

The realization hit Deirdre that there was no way to undo those past years. She had to accept the fact that she'd made a mistake. She had to survive. After several weeks of brain numbing sitcoms and bags of chocolate, Deirdre decided that she would have to take charge of her own recovery.

There were many parts to cleaning up such a mess. To tackle them as a whole was untenable. Her organizational skills and defenses kicked in. Deirdre began to set priorities, small goals and objectives. She would accomplish one small thing each day; called to cancel Jack's health insurance, cleared out one drawer of his things, wrote a letter to a debt collector. Bit by bit things got accomplished.

The food binge had added ten pounds to her frame. No, she could not, would not tackle a diet. But she did begin to change her pattern. She began to eat what she wanted, but no more junk food. She began to exercise. The first step was agony, but rather than exhausting her further, it increased her energy. Running a couple of miles a day became therapeutic in many ways.

The debts from Jack's undisclosed spending and borrowing were overwhelming. While she still couldn't bring herself to move, she decided to begin lightening her expenses in small increments. Putting an ad in the paper, she sold some of his expensive suits and exercise equipment that he never used—the rest she gave to Goodwill, cut the cable down to basic, and traded her Eldorado for a Saturn. The Cadillac was Jack's fantasy. She'd never wanted it anyway. There were many accouterments that Jack required, which Deirdre didn't need.

In order to cope with the feelings of shame and guilt, Deirdre felt she needed to give something of herself. Calling the Delaware

Council for Gambling Problems, she asked what she could do. They were quick to train her as a volunteer for the Gambling Helpline, where she offered her services to talk to family members and victims. Giving to others was extremely healing.

Deirdre began to write down her thoughts and feelings in a journal. The experience was cathartic. Sharing her experiences with others just might help them with their own survival.

Each day brought new obstacles, however. Several of Jack's clients filed a lawsuit against her to regain the money Jack took from them, money she didn't have. Many wanted her to be punished. Some still believed she belonged in prison with Jack.

With each battle, even the ones she lost, she found that she gained in strength. There was one major battle to be fought, however. The Board of Regulations was challenging her right to retain her professional license as a mental health counselor. This was her life. The license represented a lifetime of work and study. Her work was who she was as a person. The very thought of losing her sense of self, her reputation, left her feeling cold and empty. What would she do if she lost her right to practice?

JACK

Jack sat in his cell and waited for Deirdre to come to her senses. He couldn't understand why she didn't just ask their friends for the money to bail him out. He wrote her long letters explaining the situation. It was only money, after all. They could give it back and everything would be all right. Deirdre was just angry. If she could just get beyond the anger, she would be her old loving self.

After several weeks, Jack realized that Deirdre was not going to save him. The Public Defender made it clear that if he didn't plead guilty they could put him in prison for life as an habitual offender. Jack couldn't believe that Deirdre would let him go to prison. He was her soul mate.

Jack Stiles was not faring well in prison. The newspaper articles, calling him a con man, elicited constant jeers from his fellow inmates. His old friends Frank and Hawk were long gone. Frank had died of a heart attack a year ago, and Hawk had been released on a technicality.

No money had been placed in his commissary account. That bitch, Deirdre couldn't even send him a few bucks. When he received the divorce papers, he was shocked. How could she divorce him? She had even stopped taking his calls. He hated turning away from the phone to face all those knowing looks. His call had been rejected. He was a loser, they all thought.

This was her fault. She did this to him. Whatever made him think she was deserving of him?

"Hey, man," Jerry Wells, a short redhead, bellowed as he thrust the article in Jack's face. "Your old lady really did you in!"

Jack stared the man down, giving him his cold, haughty, *I'm superior* look. Eventually, Jerry moved on quoting aloud from the article.

"Dr. Warren cooperates with the Attorney General's Office in the conviction of Jack Stiles." Jerry could still be heard cackling as he moved down the hall.

Jack retreated to his cell, the article crushed in his hand. He didn't need to look at it again to see the words imprinted in his brain.

The confusion Jack had been feeling began to evolve into anger, and then rage toward Deirdre. He had saved her from a life of loneliness. He breathed meaning into her pitiful existence. He gave her love. Most of all, he gave her himself. She betrayed him. Why hadn't Deirdre come forward in his defense? Why had she betrayed him? Where were his friends, the clients who cared so much about him? The questions repeated themselves over and over without answer.

Out of sight of the other inmates, Jack smoothed the article, which included a picture of Deirdre. Taking out his pen, he began to circle the face with black arrows, his vision darkening as the rage filled his being. Finally, he drew one long black arrow across her throat, deepening it until the pen sliced through the paper.

Jack's vision then began to clear, and the dark scowl was replaced with a slow smile. Jack pulled out a clean piece of paper and an envelope, which he addressed to Mr. A. W. Houser. On the paper, Jack wrote: *Hawk, I need to see you!*

DEIRDRE

The morning was foggy and warm for October. Deirdre drove to the hearing with a heart heavy with resignation and fear. The Board of Professional Regulation would determine her future today. She was expected to defend the right to maintain her professional license as a mental health counselor.

The State would have a team of lawyers. Deirdre would be alone, representing herself. A fool for a client. She knew she should have an attorney, but the money just wasn't there. She could hear her mother's voice inside her head, *Dee, you should have known better.*

Deirdre tried in her mind to put herself in the place of the Board members. What would she do? The answer was so clear. She had not protected her clients from Jack. She should have known he would hurt someone, but she always thought it would be her. Well, today it would be.

Deirdre located the foreboding brick building without much difficulty. She was early as usual. A few people had arrived. They appeared to be clerical assistants, setting agendas and documents around a large rectangular table.

Deirdre was told by a tall, blonde woman in her thirties to sit at the far end of the table. She later learned the woman was the Chairperson. Deirdre flashed her a brief smile of thanks for the information. The smile was not returned.

Deirdre focused her attention on the large Styrofoam container of coffee she had picked up on the way. Why, she wondered, did she always add caffeine to her already frayed nerves?

The Board members filed into the room. A man in his sixties, with thinning brown hair, and a too tight suit, gave her a brief, stern glare and sat down. Another man, thirtyish, with a sandy ponytail, khaki pants, and a navy sport coat smiled warmly at her. A woman with white hair, and a face lined with her own years of pain, glanced at Deirdre sympathetically, and then, as though Deirdre's presence made her uncomfortable, looked away. The remaining two members, a fiftyish woman in a business suit, and another woman with short, cropped hair, wearing casual slacks and a polo shirt, pointedly ignored her.

They began discussing other business while awaiting the final member who would provide a quorum. When he arrived, a heavy-set man in his late fifties, with a steel gray crew cut, dark suite, white sox and loafers, the hearing began.

Deirdre took a deep breath, coughed, and began her opening statement. Fortunately, she was allowed to remain seated. Her knees felt too weak to allow her to stand for very long. She had only begun when her statement was abruptly halted.

"Dr. Warren, you will have to speak up. We can't hear you from this end of the table." Deirdre could not see the face attached to the brittle female voice.

"Would it help if I moved to the witness chair at the end of the table?" she offered.

They all agreed and Deirdre shifted her position and began again. Her statement was six pages long. Deirdre knew that she should be brief, but felt that it was necessary to provide the Board with background into her relationship with Jack. How could they possibly understand what was so incomprehensible?

As Deirdre described her relationship with Jack and his explanations for the lies, her own awareness deepened. All the warning signs she had ignored flashed in front of her. Why, she asked herself, had she not heeded them? She glanced up at the Board members periodically and studied their faces. Their looks were disdainful, some hostile.

The man with the thinning brown hair rolled his eyes in disbelief. There were no looks of sympathy. There would be no compassion or understanding from this group.

What would you think if you were listening to this drivel? Deirdre asked herself.

Her heart was not in her defense. She saw her own weaknesses related to Jack Stiles reflected in front of her, and she didn't like herself one bit.

Deirdre concluded her statement like a slowly deflating balloon.

The prosecutor, however, was not lacking in energy or enthusiasm. She was the champion of Jack Stiles' victims. Dr. Deirdre Warren had aided and abetted the enemy. She deserved to be punished.

Erin Shanahan was the daughter of an Irish cop. He had lost his life defending an elderly woman from a mugger. As Casey Shanahan had struggled with the mugger, the man had taken the cop's weapon from its holster and shot him. Help came in time to stop the mugger, but not in time to save her father's life.

Erin had been educated with the money her mother had received from her father's insurance. Shanahan had bought extra life insurance, struggling to meet the premiums, as though he knew his life would be terminated before his only child, his precious Erin, could be educated properly.

Erin grew up with a fire in her belly. She was driven to eradicate evil, or the support of evil, in any manner. Erin Shanahan was a powerful force.

Deirdre watched her opponent with an admiration she could not contain. She and Erin were actually kindred spirits. Deirdre's father had been a narcotics investigator who was killed in a roadblock organized to stop two teenage cop killers on a rampage through California. The difference was that Deirdre had always felt her father could have lived if he had shot to kill, rather than to arrest.

Harley Warren had started the first boys' club in the small California town where Deirdre was raised. As dedicated as he was to law and order, he was convinced that everyone needed a fair chance at life. Before he became a detective, Warren had been an unruly kid.

He could easily have gone in another direction if it had not been for a police athletic league volunteer who had taken him under his wing.

Deirdre grew up wanting to give the underdog the benefit of the doubt. As a teenager, her classmates labeled her a do-gooder. She always befriended kids that weren't allowed into the special cliques.

Justice, however, was the key to Deirdre's existence. Jack Stiles had conned Deirdre, but she had allowed it to happen. Erin Shanahan was on the side of justice. Deirdre watched the dark-eyed, curly haired prosecutor and knew that this woman would be the victor today.

As the prosecution's witnesses poured forth, Deirdre felt an insurgence of the guilt and shame she had suffered when Jack had first been arrested. She had allowed a convicted felon to counsel people who did not have the benefit of knowing his history. He had coerced money from them by pretending that he was providing an investment opportunity, which would give them a forty percent return on their money.

Several waitresses came forward to describe how Jack had paid restaurant checks with hundred dollar bills, and had called himself "Dr. Stiles." Deirdre recalled the many arguments she'd had with Jack.

"I worked hard for that title," she would argue. "You can't just appropriate it as though it were your right."

"My love," he had responded, "what are titles? They mean nothing. It is mere folly. Don't be so upset."

"Just don't ever do it with our clients."

"Of course, not. That is different. You know I would never do such a thing," he scoffed indignantly.

When it came time for Erin to cross-examine Deirdre, she was completely unprepared. A large file was placed in front of her.

"Do you recognize the documents in this file?"

The file contained a stack of forged documents, including insurance forms, letters to agencies, and statements with DSM Diagnostic Codes. They carried Deirdre's signature. Jack had signed her name to all the documents in the file.

Deirdre felt sick. She had never seen any of these forms before.

"These documents were in the files found in Jack Stiles office. If you had taken the time to review these files, you would have seen them."

Deirdre flashed on the frequent clashes with Jack over the files.

What are you doing? He would ask.

I'm reviewing the files.

Why?

Why not? I am your supervisor.

You're my wife. Don't you trust my work yet?

That's not the point, Jack. I'm supposed to do this..

Do it later. I'm working on notes, now. I don't want my work mixed up.

Deirdre had always felt overloaded. There were never enough hours. She always knew she should insist, but she was too tired to argue. She gave in to Jack. She always gave in to Jack. When she did look at the files, there was nothing awry. Of course, those were the files he had hidden.

Deirdre was so overwhelmed by the new information that she was unable to respond to Erin's questions. Why didn't she review the files? How could she explain? Who would understand? Deirdre didn't understand it herself. She shook her head.

When Erin concluded her arguments, Deirdre was surprised to discover that she would be allowed to remain in the room while the Board deliberated.

"It's an open hearing. You may remain," they told her.

Deirdre did just that. But it was one of the most humiliating experiences of her life. They spoke of protecting society from Dr. Deirdre Warren and quickly determined that her license should be revoked. Deirdre left the room in a daze.

Deirdre knew in her heart that she did not know Jack was capable of such evil, but she also knew that she had invited him onto her ship. As Captain of that ship, she was responsible for its passengers, and Jack Stiles had brought a virus aboard that had destroyed the very occupants she was sworn to protect. His violation of them was her responsibility. She should have protected them. She should have known.

As Deirdre drove away from the hearing, she felt the pain, which she'd first experienced as an intense blow to the solar plexus, begin to spread through her chest. She began to shake until she feared she would not be able to control the wheel. Then, pulling to the side of the road, she allowed the sobs to erupt without control.

For nearly an hour Deirdre vented her anguish, anger, and agony, unnoticed by the frenetic commuters, rushing to begin their weekends. Slowly, she regained control and began the drive home.

Through her pain she realized the drizzle had ended, and a faint rainbow edged the horizon. Would she finally be able to heal? Most of all, would she finally be able to forgive herself?

JACK

The night before he was to be sentenced, Jack prepared himself. He would convince them that he was in the right. He had helped people, after all. They would get their money back eventually. He would make them see.

Jack Stiles walked slowly up to the witness stand. He cleared his throat twice, took a deep breath, and gazed belligerently out at the onlookers.

"Where is the justice in this court?" he declared in a loud but calm voice. He looked into the eyes of each of his victims, carefully, one by one. "You all know the truth? You know I helped you. What is money compared to that? You know the truth, and I know the truth." He seemed almost to threaten the group.

Jack flipped through pages on a yellow pad and then turned to the judge. Judge Martin looked up with no expression as Jack referred to the late U.S. Supreme Court Justice Oliver Wendell Holmes and declared, "You must not react to the abject pain and anger the victims are feeling, but sentence me according to the law. What has been said, your Honor lacks the full declaration of truth."

Jack gathered up his papers and walked back to his position at the defense table.

A man asked, "How was the surgery?"

A woman yelled, "You are a bad, bad man."

Others derisively shouted "Bravo!"

Jack stopped when he reached the table and looked at the hecklers in confusion. These were his worshipers, his flock. How could they turn on him? They all knew how special he was. None of this was important.

The prosecutor stood up and declared, "The people of this State are not safe if Jack Stiles is on the street."

The judge then asked Jack to stand. He looked at Jack for a full moment before he began. "I have little patience with men like you, Jack Stiles. With what you said today, you continue to hurt these people. You seem to have no remorse for what you have done. You have made a lifestyle out of harming others. You deserve the maximum sentence. Jack Stiles I sentence you to twelve years, plus fifteen years probation. The entire twelve years is to be served in prison."

Jack felt stunned as he was led from the room. His eyes sought out Deirdre. This is your fault, the look said. The hatred in his eyes was undisguised this time. Back in his cell, the sentence continued to ring in his head. This was no longer temporary.

DEIRDRE

Deirdre couldn't move. She heard a loud roaring noise in her ears, and realized it was the sound of cheering. The courtroom had erupted when the judge read the sentence. Deirdre spotted the other women. They all sat quietly among the commotion, each caught in her own, private reflection. As the reality hit her, she began to smile. Pleased. Now she would have some closure.

Leaving the courtroom, however, she spotted a man who had been looking at her all morning. He nodded and grinned as though he knew her. Then he mouthed the words, "watch out." When she looked again, he was gone.

Deirdre walked to her car with a strange mixture of emotions, relief, satisfaction, and she had to admit. fear. Trying to shake the latter she kept telling herself, he couldn't hurt her from jail.

But what happens when he gets out?

EPILOGUE

It had been nearly a year since Jack's arrest, and Deirdre was finally beginning to heal. At the advice of her therapist, she had stopped reading the long, accusatory letters that Jack inflicted upon her weekly. Not yet able to destroy the letters, she kept them all in a box. As she opened the box to insert the latest installment, she experienced a foul sensation. She quickly covered the box and moved it to a seldom-used closet. Maybe it was time to throw them out.

Next to the box of Jack's letters was a pile of Julie's diaries. Deirdre was boxing them up to ship to California, at Julie's request.

Deirdre's first conversation with Julie had been prompted by Julie's fury.

"How dare you read my diaries." Someone had anonymously sent Julie a copy of one of the newspaper articles. The article referred to the diaries Deirdre had turned over to the Attorney General's Office.

"Please listen to me," Deirdre pleaded. *"I thought you were dead."*

Julie's hostility soon turned to sympathy. "The diaries didn't say everything," Julie admitted. *"It took me ten years to realize that I was terrified of Jack. There is something evil about him."*

"But you loved him so much."

"Deirdre, I don't think it was love. I was in his spell. He does that to people. He almost destroyed me. Whatever you do, don't let him know where I am."

"No, I promise."

Thinking of that phone conversation, the feeling of uneasiness she'd been experiencing over the past week returned. She kept remembering the psychiatrist's report.

"This man has a criminal mind, Dr. Warren. He could be dangerous under the right circumstances."

"That's not possible. Jack never so much as raised his voice to me in seven years.

"No, his aggression is much more subtle. Take my professional advice, though. Stay away from him."

That conversation had taken place nearly a year ago, and Deirdre had heeded his advice. She had not seen Jack Stiles since that day in court. Nevertheless, the uneasiness increased. She couldn't identify the source. It was more than just a residue of the past year. A new and unbidden feeling had emerged. Unable to find a reason for her discomfiture, she busied herself with a new article on gambling she had been writing.

When the call came from one of Jack's friends, she wasn't surprised. Many people attempted to help Jack since his arrest, clergy, and counselors. Jack would send them to her to pick up items, posters, and books. She would give them what he had requested, and offer them coffee and conversation. They were always surprised that she wasn't more vengeful.

"Jack says you are overwhelmed with anger," they all said. "He claims that, when you get beyond the anger, you will remember how much you love him, and become the old Deirdre again."

Deirdre would explain patiently. *How can you be angry at a rattlesnake when it bites you? It is its nature. I am angry with myself for not seeing his true nature before he hurt so many people.*

Jack's emissaries would leave, confused. Jack had portrayed a vengeful woman, spewing venom at every opportunity in her desire to hurt him.

Today the call was similar to the others. The man spoke so softly she could barely hear him. Jack had asked him to pick up a book of poetry.

"I know the book you mean," Deirdre answered, "but I think I gave it to him months ago. I'll check."

"Can I come now?" the man asked.

"But I'm not sure the book is here."

"That's okay. I have something Jack wanted me to give you."

"Oh, I guess that's all right. Can you give me an hour?"

"One hour." The caller hung up.

Deirdre shivered. The uneasiness returned.

Just sixty minutes later the doorbell rang. Deirdre escorted the man upstairs to the living area. As she reached the top of the stairs she asked, "What did you say your name was?"

"They just call me Hawk."

AFTERWORD

How many people can say that they have never gambled, never purchased a lottery ticket, played bingo, cards, or bet on their golf games? According to the National Council on Problem Gambling revenues from legal wagering in the United States have grown by nearly 1,500%. By 1995, the amount wagered legally in the United States had reached $550 billion or 9% of United States personal income. An individual can make a legal wager in every state except Utah and Hawaii. There are over 700 casinos in operation in twenty-eight states (January 1997).

Not everyone is a pathological gambler. Many may gamble recreationally, spending money as they would on an evening of entertainment. Others are professional gamblers, wagering with cool calculation. But there is no calm connected to the pathological gambler. This individual is out of control like a toboggan going downhill without a rider.

Once gambling was perceived as a weakness or as sinful. However, gambling is now recognized as a disease. The main features of this disease are that the pathological gambler is emotionally dependent, having lost control over the impulse to gamble. The behavior interferes with normal activities and usually destroys their personal lives. The DSM-IV (Diagnostic and Statistical Manual of Mental Disorders, 4th Edition) categorizes pathological gambling as an Impulse Control Disorder (American Psychiatric Association, 1994). The criteria for Pathological Gambling are:

Persistent and recurrent maladaptive gambling behavior as indicated by five (or more) of the following:

1. is preoccupied with gambling, handicapping or planning their next venture or thinking of ways to get money with which to gamble.
2. needs to gamble with increasing amounts of money in order to achieve the desired excitement
3. has repeated unsuccessful efforts to control, cut back or stop gambling
4. is restless or irritable when attempting to cut down or stop gambling
5. gambles as a way of escaping from problems or if relieving a dysphoric mood
6. after losing money, often returns another day to get even (called chasing).
7. lies to family members, therapist, or others to conceal the extent of involvement with gambling
8. has committed illegal acts such as forgery, fraud, theft or embezzlement to finance gambling
9. has jeopardized or lost a significant relationship, job or educational or career opportunity because of gambling.
10. relies on others to provide money to relieve a desperate financial situation caused by gambling.

Characteristics associated with pathological gambling include high achievement, exhibitionism, dominance and endurance. However, pathological gamblers are more likely than the average person to be sociopaths (currently identified by the DSM-IV as Antisocial Personality Disorders). This is an individual who lacks personal loyalties, shows poor judgment and responsibility and is capable of rationalizing or justifying inappropriate behavior.

Another personality disorder association with pathological gambling is Narcissism. The Narcissist lacks empathy for others, has a pattern of grandiosity and a strong need for admiration (American

Psychiatric Association). The narcissist has a sense of entitlement, and often resents the success of others. The degree of narcissism, as with other disorders, varies. On the low end of the spectrum, the individual may be merely self involved, a Peter Pan, who takes no responsibility for his life. However, in its severe form, the narcissist may become delusional, believing himself to be a superior being who is beyond the rules and mores of society. He may be full of rage at those who have what he feels he deserves. This individual will do anything to satisfy his need for superiority.

Depression is also very common among pathological gamblers. One theory is that pathological gamblers have lower levels of naturally occurring epinephrine and norepinephrine in the brain and require more stimulation than the average individual.

An article in Comprehensive Psychiatry (McElroy, et al, 1996) questions whether pathological gambling is related to bipolar Disorders. Bipolar Disorders involve alternating periods of mania or hypomania and depression. There is a similarity in family history, biology, and treatment response between pathological gamblers and those with bipolar disorders, formerly referred to as manic-depression.

Two components are associated with Pathological Gambling, action and chasing (Lesieur, 1993). Action relates to the thrill-seeking, risk-taking way of life. Chasing combines poor money management and a desire to get even after heavy losses. The state of arousal produced by gambling becomes as addictive as a drug.

The addiction component of gambling often crosses other habits such as alcohol and drugs. The addictions are often combined, such as drinking while gambling. For others one becomes a substitution. The abstinent alcoholic may turn to gambling.

According to Dr. Robert L. Custer there are three phases of gambling: the winning phase, the losing phase and the desperation phase. During the winning phase there is excitement and promise. Usually a big win. The gambler becomes convinced that he is smarter and luckier than others. Some use this phase as a way to escape problems, financial or emotional.

During the losing phase the chase is on. Continued gambling brings increasing loses and borrowing money. Urgency becomes so intense that the gambler may engage in illegal activities. If the pathological gambler also suffers from Anti-social or Narcissistic Personality Disorders then the illegal activities are easily rationalized and may include fraud or con games. Family problems increase and the gambler's personal life begins to unravel.

The final phase, the desperation phase is the end of the line, a form of panic when one runs out of options. The spouse leaves, one loses a job or may be arrested. Sometimes suicide is considered. Many gamblers reach the desperation phase several times before they hit *low bottom*. Low bottom is a term used by Gambler's Anonymous, which was developed in 1957, to mean when you've gone as low as you can get. You've lost everything, face prison, have nothing left.

The Gamblers Anonymous 'COMBO' book describes the world of the compulsive gambler as a dream world in which a lot of time is spent creating images of the great and wonderful things they are going to do as soon as they make the big win. When they win, they gamble to dream still greater dreams. But when failing, "they gamble in reckless desperation and the depths of their misery are fathomless as their dream world comes crashing down. Sadly, they will struggle back, dream more dreams, and, of course, suffer more misery. No one can convince them that their great schemes will not some day come true. They believe they will, for without this dream world, life for them would not be tolerable." pp10-11.

While the names and some of the details in the story you have just read have been changed to protect the privacy of the people involved, the story is based on true experiences. The man portrayed in this story hit low bottom on August 2, 1996, exactly seven years after he met his last victim. He was diagnosed with. pathological gambling and severe narcissistic personality disorder, and given a twelve-year prison sentence for fraud. He is currently attempting to have his sentence reviewed. When asked what he plans to do after his release, he states that he plans to be a psychotherapist.

REFERENCES

American Psychiatric Association. (1994) Diagnostic and Statistical Manual of Mental Disorders. Washington, D.C.

Beck, A.T., Rush, A.J., Shaw, B.F. & Emery, G. (1979) Cognitive Therapy of Depression. New York: The Guilford Press

Bergler, Edmund (1985). The Psychology of Gambling. USA: International Uni- versities Press, Inc.

Berman, L. and Seigel, M. (1992). Behind the 8-Ball: A Guide for Families of Gamblers, New York: Fireside/Parkside

Birnbaum, K. (1914). Die Psychopathischen Verbrecker, 2nd Ed. Leipzig: Thieme.

Blaszcynski, Alex and Silove, Derrick. (Summer, 1995) Cognitive and behavior therapies for pathological gambling. Journal of Gambling studies 11:195-220.

Ciarrocchi, J. & Richardson, R. (1980). Profile of compulsive gamblers in treatment: update and comparisons. Journal of Gambling Behavior, 5(1), 53-65.

Cleckley, H. M. (1964). The Mask of Sanity, 4th Ed. St. Louis: C. V. Mosby.

Crockford, D.N (1998). Naltrexone in the treatment of pathological gambling and alcohol dependence. Canadian Journal of Psychiatry, 43(1), 86.

Custer, R. L. and Milt, H. (1985) <u>When Luck Runs Out: Help for Compulsive Gamblers and their Families</u>. New York: Warner Brothers.

Dostoevsky, Fydor (1966) <u>The Gambler</u>. Great Britain: Hazell Watson & Viney, Ltd.

Frankl, Viktor E. (1959) <u>Man's Search for Meaning</u>. New York: Simon & Schuster, Inc.

Gamblers Anonymous (1984). <u>Sharing Recovery Through Gamblers Anonymous</u>. Los Angeles: Gamblers Anonymous.

Gamblers Anonymous (1991). <u>What is GA?</u> Minn.: Hazelden Educational Mate- rials.

Gamblers Anonymous (1998) Los Angeles: Gamblers Anonymous.

Gardner J. (March, 1986). The relationship between conscious and unconscious processes and individual creativity. Invited Address, California State Psychological Association Convention, San Francisco.

Harpur, Timothy J, Hart, Stephen D. and Hare, Robert D. (1994). Personality of the psychopath. In <u>Personality Disorders and the Five-Factor Model of Personality</u>.

Costa, Paul T., Ed. Washington, D. C: American Psychological Association.

Heineman, Mary (1992). <u>Losing Your Shirt</u>. Center City, Minnesota: Hazeldon.

Horney, K. (1945). <u>Our Inner Conflicts</u>. New York: Norton.

Humphrey, S. H. and Walsh, J. M. (June 1998). Assessment and Treatment of Gambling disorders in a Community Mental Health center. Paper presented at the National Conference on Problem Gambling. Las Vegas, Nevada.

Humphrey, Hale (November, 2000). This Must Be Hell: A look at pathological gambling. New York: Writer's Club Press.

Humphrey, Hale & Slawik, Melvin. (October 2000). The Three Faces of Narcissism. Paper presented at the National Conference on Problem Gambling. Phila- delphia, PA.

Kernberg, O. (1975). Borderline Conditions and Pathological Narcissism. New York: Jason Aronson.

Lesieur, Henry R. (1984) The Chase. Rochester, VT: Schenkman Books, Inc.

Lesieur, H.R. & Blume, S.B. (1987). The South Oaks Gambling Screen (SOGS): A new instrument for the identification of pathological gamblers. American Journal of Psychiatry, 41, 1009-1012.

Lilienfeld, S. O. (1990). Conceptual and empirical issues in the assesment of psychopathology. Unpublished Manuscript.

Meloy, J. Reid (1988). The Psychopathiic Mind: Origins, Dynamics, and Treatment. London: Jason Aronson, Inc.

Miller, Wm. R. & Rollnick, S. (1991). Motivational Interviewing: Preparing People to Change Addictive Behavior. New York: Guildford Press.

Prichard, J. C. (1835). A Treatise on Insanity. Trans. D. Davis. New York: Hafner.

Prochaska, J. O., & DiClemente, C. C. (1986). Toward a comprehensive model of change. In W. R. Miller & N. Heather (Eds.) <u>Treating Addictive Behaviors:</u>

<u>Processes of Change</u>, (pp. 3-27) New York: Plenum Press.

Siegel, Mary Ellen and Berman, Linda (1992). <u>Behind the 8-Ball</u>. New York: Fireside/Parkside Simon and Schuster.

Milton Keynes UK
Ingram Content Group UK Ltd.
UKHW022132291124
451915UK00010B/644